DEATH'S REACH

Mary was so lost in her thoughts on the comparative merits of May Green and Wildesham flora that she hadn't noticed that Dog had disappeared. Moments before, he had been diving and lurching through the undergrowth ahead of her and now he seemed to have vanished. She stopped and listened. There was nothing. No wind, not even the sound of a car on the road that came around the valley. Only silence. Mary felt her spine tingle.

"Dog?" she called rather feebly. "Dog?" She felt rather stupid standing there on the footpath shouting "Dog." Normally, Mary wouldn't have minded too much. But today she was in a hurry and she didn't have time to play games.

"Damn!" she said out loud. And then, as she began to move forward, she was rewarded with the sound of snuffling. She followed the noise, picking her way through the prickly undergrowth until she could see the black shape of Dog. He was obviously going to be obstinate. When Mary called him he turned and grinned at her over his shoulder. Holding the leash menacingly, she went after Dog.

There appeared to be nothing at all in the pile of underbrush and brambles that he was investigating. She couldn't understand what it was that he had found that could possibly be so fascinating. It was not until she leaned over and got hold of him, not until she bent down to clip the lead onto his collar, that she saw, inches away from her face, a human hand. . . .

THE KILLING OF ELLIS MARTIN

LUCRETIA GRINDLE

POCKET BOOKS

New York London Toronto Sydney Tokyo Singapore

This book is a work of fiction. Names, characters, places and incidents are either products of the author's imagination or are used fictitiously. Any resemblance to actual events or locales or persons, living or dead, is entirely coincidental.

An *Original* Publication of POCKET BOOKS

POCKET BOOKS, a division of Simon & Schuster Inc.
1230 Avenue of the Americas, New York, NY 10020

ISBN: 0-671-74845-9

First Pocket Books printing June 1993

10 9 8 7 6 5 4 3 2 1

POCKET and colophon are registered trademarks of Simon & Schuster Inc.

Cover art and design by Marc Burckhardt

Printed in the U.S.A.

THE KILLING OF ELLIS MARTIN

The wind shifted, moving through the bare trees. The storm had been predicted for some time, and it came in a first sharp squall moving along the ridge. Later the wind would pick up and the storm would break, drenching the valley in long-overdue February rain. Now the leaves shifted in Tinker Wood, moving restlessly as if the earth underneath were alive and heaving. The hand was very white against the damp earth of the wood. The pile of leaves and mulch that had been covering it had shifted back and now, palm upward, it seemed to be reaching out, its stiff cold fingers pointing up to the sky.

Chapter

1.

It was sometime after four o'clock when Mary Jepp started out for the May Green postbox. She thought of her husband Sam. How very like him to have left the gas bill, all sealed and ready to be posted, lying in the drawer of the front hall chest. Fat load of good it would do there. It was a lucky thing that she'd found it at all, and that had only been because she'd been looking for a spare set of car keys. Clearly Sam had left it there when he'd picked up his gloves on his way out in the morning. But which morning, and how long ago?

Mary had a horror of bureaucracy. She liked to avoid it whenever possible and avoiding it meant, in part, having the bills paid on time. She couldn't bear the thought of having to ring up the Gas Board, groveling and explaining to one unsympathetic person after another about how her husband had left the bill in a drawer and "blah, blah, blah." And would they please not turn the heating off, because usually she

3

was a responsible citizen and helped with the church flowers and bought charity Christmas cards and didn't beat her children with a horse whip?—at least not often.

At the same time that all of this was going through her mind, Mary contemplated leaving the bill until Monday and making Sam post it on his way to work. Then she rebuked herself for laziness and sloth and a catalog of other sins and told herself that it was five past four on a Friday afternoon and that if she'd just stop being so pathetic she could post the bill by four-thirty, catch the last collection, and give Dog a walk at the same time.

Mary Jepp was tall and dark and, though by no means a Vogue-cover-girl-beauty, she looked considerably younger than her forty-two years. Mary was blessed with thin hips, long legs, a generous mouth, and eyes of such a deep brown that the pupils were almost undiscernible from the irises. Dog was also tall and dark and as they set out from the house they were a matching pair: a welly-booted witch and her canine familiar.

Mary paused at the top of the hill. She wasn't certain whether to go down to the May Green postbox in the valley or cross the ridge up to the main one—if you could call it that—in Wildesham. May Green was smaller and might not have a late night collection, but it was also closer. Calling to Dog, Mary set out down the footpath that led through Tinker Wood and to the village of May Green beyond.

Away to her left, Mary could just make out the slanted tile roof of The Snipe. For centuries the tiny pub had sat at the end of the lane that ran up into Tinker Wood. It was a convenient stopping place for poachers, wanderers, and farmers. She had never cared for the place. When she and Sam felt the need for a pint of bitter they went to The Royal Oak in Wildesham, where shiny carriage brasses hung above the fireplace. The publican always had mulled wine in the winter. Sam occasionally said that The Royal Oak was a bit naff and it was true that the publican came from London, bringing his good taste with him. But Mary didn't care; she liked it anyways. Dog made a crashing sound in the woods ahead of her and Mary whistled for him and turned away from The Snipe into Tinker Wood.

Ordinarily, Mary liked woods, their silence and the rustle of leaves and the smooth bark of the trees and the way the light fell through them. But she didn't like Tinker Wood. There was something about it that had always seemed rather grotty and vaguely frightening. The trees were scrubby and close together and the undergrowth and brambles grew in a thick tangled mass. Sam had once explained to her that this was because of the kind of wood it was, something to do with the trees and that the soil was different here from the other side of the valley where the old Roman road ran through lovely forests of beech and oak. When the children were small, Mary had walked with them along the Roman road and told them stories of knights in armor and lovely ladies and kind old wizards appearing from behind tree trunks.

Certainly no wizards here, Mary thought as she went down the narrow path. There was, in fact, not so much as a hint of magic in this wood. Not even bad magic. This was the sort of horrid little modern wood where you half expect men in raincoats to lurk about waiting to expose themselves. Not that anything of that kind had ever happened in Wildesham. The idea was so bizarre as to be funny. But then again, Mary reminded herself, this was not Wildesham proper. It was May Green and there was a difference. The woods proved it.

Mary was so lost in her thoughts on the comparative merits of May Green and Wildesham flora that it took her some time to notice Dog's disappearance. Moments before he had been diving and lurching through the undergrowth ahead of her and now he seemed to have vanished. She stopped and listened. There was no wind, not even the sound of a car on the road that came around the valley. Only silence. Mary felt her spine go all tingly. She told herself that it was nothing more than irritation and not some sinister foreboding that she felt. She stood there fingering the envelope in her pocket.

"Dog?" she called rather feebly. "Dog?" She felt rather stupid standing there on the footpath shouting "Dog." The dog did, in fact, have a name. The twins had called it Bluebell. Mary found this name so demeaning for a male black labrador that it was more than she could bring herself to do to use it. Instead she just called him Dog, which he seemed to like just as well.

After a few more tries Dog had still not appeared. Normally, Mary wouldn't have minded too much. But today she was in a hurry and she didn't have time to play games with stupid Dog.

"Damn!" she said out loud. "Damn Dog!" And then, as she began to move forward, she noticed a path leading up to the left. Mary knew where this path went. It was actually a disused drive, quite a large track that cut across the footpath up to an abandoned cottage. The small boarded-up building was inside the wood, near the boundary to the Grainger farm. For as long as Mary had known, it had sat in these grotty woods with the clearing growing in and around it. It was a nasty-looking place and the twins had strict instructions not to play near it, which probably made it all the more attractive. Mary started up the old drive, cursing Dog as she went.

As she stood beside the cottage, she was rewarded with the sound of snuffling. She followed the noise, picking her way through the prickly undergrowth until she could see the black shape of Dog ahead of her. He was obviously going to be obstinate. When Mary called him he turned and grinned at her over his shoulder and went on snuffling happily. Despite the fact that he had most likely found a particularly interesting rabbit hole or even a badger set, Mary was in no mood to indulge him. Holding the leash menacingly, she went after Dog.

There appeared to be nothing at all in the pile of underbrush and brambles that he was investigating. She couldn't understand what it was that he had found that could possibly be so fascinating. It was not until she leaned over and got ahold of him, not until she bent down to clip the lead onto his collar, that she saw, inches away from her face, a human hand.

It was 4:36 P.M. on Friday, February eleventh, when Constable Barry Glen answered the telephone at Millbrook police station and heard a woman report that she had found a body in Tinker Wood. Constable Glen later remembered that she sounded quite calm and composed as she gave him her name and address. She was only a little breathless and she apologized for that, explaining that she had just run all the way home. After telling her that they would be with her directly, Constable Glen put the telephone down and felt a thrill of excitement. In the last five years nothing more interesting than a stolen Ford Capri and graffiti on the train station wall had happened around here. Perhaps, at last, something was going to break.

After phoning the police Mary stood very still in the middle of the kitchen. She noticed that her muddy boots had left tracks across the stone floor and she took them off and stood them by the kitchen door. Then she locked the door. Then she ran from room to room locking all of the doors and latching all of the windows. When she was absolutely certain that the house was completely locked she went back into the kitchen and sat on the floor in front of the large Swedish Aga stove with her arm around the comforting lump of Dog.

Mary Jepp was very frightened. In the woods, not half an hour ago, she had seen a human hand which was very clearly dead. Attached to that hand would be an arm and attached to that arm would be the rest of the body, a body that was buried. Someone was dead and dead bodies didn't bury themselves in Tinker Wood. Mary Jepp understood quite clearly that whoever had buried the body there had had a reason for doing so and that reason was probably murder.

When Sam Jepp got home from his office in Tunbridge Wells at half past six he was surprised and then alarmed to see two police cars parked in his front drive. He was even more alarmed when a policewoman opened the door to his house while he was still halfway up the front steps and told him that his wife was in the kitchen. And there she was, making coffee for three other policemen who seemed to be holding some sort of convention around the Aga. Dog looked up at Sam and grinned, thumping his tail.

"Mary? Is it the twins?" asked Sam. Mary turned and saw him standing in the doorway. She was still holding the kettle.

"The twins are fine," she said quickly, "but thank God you're here. The most horrible thing has happened." And then she told him about Tinker Wood.

By evening the news was all over the village. There were an awful lot of police at the Jepp house and even more streamed throughout Tinker Wood. People were saying that on her way to the postbox that afternoon, Mary Jepp had found a body. The words "murder" and "suicide" traveled along the telephone lines as well as the information that it was a tramp or an unidentified woman or two teenagers from London in a tragic love-suicide-death pact. The local reporter was favoring the last theory, but in fact, no one knew who it was, not even Mary Jepp.

Up at Tinker Wood there were police cars and lights and a good deal of orange tape that was being strung from tree to tree to keep out the curious. But still no one knew who was at the center of all of this attention. Mary Jepp had already explained to several friends who had rung to see if she was "all right" that she had no idea if there was even a body. What she had seen was a hand. Everything else, if there was anything else, was covered in leaves and mulch and earth. She certainly hadn't seen a face.

Just after dawn the next day Chief Inspector Ross stood looking down at the face. It was the face of a girl who had once been very pretty. She had had long blond hair and small, even features. He couldn't tell what color her eyes had been, but he bet they were blue. She was wearing a barbour jacket, still zipped to the throat, corduroy trousers and leather slip-on shoes. This murderer had had a sense of propriety; an expensive silk scarf, with a pattern of a tiger's face looking out of jungle leaves spread across it, had been placed, shroudlike, across her face before she was buried. Already forensics had removed it, sealing it carefully into a plastic bag and labeling it in order that it could be entered into a complicated catalog of numbered references that had already become this girl's new identity.

When the body was removed and handed over to pathology they would be able to tell him what had killed her, but for now Ross presumed it was the blow that had left a livid gash across the side of her head. It would probably turn out to have been done with some kind of heavy, edged instrument, perhaps even the same shovel that had been used to dig the rather shallow grave. It didn't look as though there was "sexual interference," as they so quaintly called it, but you could never tell. Forensics would know soon enough. Ross wondered whether he would ever get used to looking at dead bodies. On the whole he hoped not. He turned away from the grave.

He had come up to Tinker Wood last night as soon as he had gotten the call. May Green was only a half hour from his home on the coast. When he arrived, the area had already been cordoned off by the local police. A small throng of the curious had gathered by the edge of the wood along with the crime reporter from the local rag who was one of Ross's least favorite young men. Ross had walked past the crowd, past the cottage, to the place where the body had been buried. A plastic cover had been erected over the grave and the surrounding area. The trees and surrounding undergrowth were eerily lit with floodlights and hung with fluorescent tape as if for some surrealist woodland festival.

A few minutes later Ross had walked back to the meadow at the edge of the wood. He was a tall, thin man whose rather ordinary face was distinguished only by a pair of very blue eyes. With his unsmiling countenance and long-fingered, elegant hands he might have been a pianist or a painter, an actor or a diplomat, almost anything, in fact, except a policeman. But a policeman he was, a senior Chief Inspector whose chosen specialty was homicide and last night, having taken control of the investigation now underway in Tinker Wood, Ross made his first statement concerning the case. Standing in the glare of the police lights he announced that nothing would happen until the following morning at first light. After that he had driven home, said a small prayer that there would not be rain, and had gone to sleep. The thought of a new investigation exhausted him.

Now, just after 7:00 A.M. on February twelfth, the wood was a buzzing hive of activity. All the apparatus of a murder investigation had fallen neatly into place. The body had been painstakingly uncovered and the area was being swept minutely for any kind of material evidence. The police photographers were recording the entire spectacular event on film. Everything that could be done was being done to make Ross's job as simple and straightforward as possible. He had every available resource to fall back on. All he had to do was work out who had killed her.

Right now, however, what he needed was a positive identification. Her pockets had been empty except for a few old tissues and a cheaply laminated card that read "Millbrook Video Center" across the top. Underneath the name "E. Martin" had been typed in and below that there was an incomprehensible signature.

As Ross came down to the field that ran up to the edge of the wood he saw a mass of people standing on the far side of the orange tape and felt a great deal of pity for the farmer who owned the land. This field was planted and, due to the unseasonably mild weather, had a nicely advanced crop of winter wheat on it. Or rather it once had. The wheat was now firmly in the past tense. It had been trampled into the heavy Kent clay by the police, the villagers, and even a local television crew. Looking at the assorted group, Ross couldn't help wondering if the murderer were among them. Would he be pleased? Would he be frightened? Why "he"? It could just as easily be a woman, couldn't it? What was important for the moment, however, was the video card which he held carefully in its plastic bag.

Mary and Sam Jepp were standing at the edge of the crowd. One of the police sergeants stood beside them while they talked to a black-haired young man wearing a barbour and wellingtons. The Jepps were wearing barbours and wellingtons as well, and so, for that matter, thought Ross, was almost everyone else, including the television crew, who had clearly decided to go native for the occasion. Well, Ross thought, who could blame them? With the exception of the announcement of a local by-election, this was the most fun they'd had in years. He ducked under the orange tape and began to make his way toward the Jepps. He had asked them to be here. Nine times out of ten the person who found the body could identify it. Eight times out of ten they were the murderer. From what he had already seen, Ross was virtually certain that this case would be an exception to the second rule. He was hoping that it would be consistent with the first. He touched Sam Jepp lightly on the shoulder and asked if he could have a word. Sam nodded and followed Ross under the orange tape and into the woods.

There had been complete silence as the two of them had left the crowd. Ross could feel the eyes of the assembled multitude on their backs. The vultures waited with baited breath. Ross held the plastic bag containing the video card out to Sam Jepp.

"Does this name mean anything to you, Mr. Jepp?" Sam looked at the card for a moment without touching it, then he looked up at Ross and nodded.

"I should think it's Ellis Martin," he said, "a local woman from Wildesham."

"Do you know how I would contact her next of kin?"

"You won't," Sam said, "because there isn't one. Ellis had no family that I know of."

"I see," Ross said, putting the card back into his pocket.

"Chief Inspector," Sam Jepp said quietly, "if you are asking me to make a positive identification, if it is Ellis, I can do that." Ross looked at him for a moment.

"You have no legal obligation, Mr. Jepp."

"I am aware of that." The two men faced one

another for a moment before Ross nodded and turned up the path toward the cottage.

"Wait!" The call came from behind and they turned to see Mary Jepp hurrying to join them.

"You don't have to do this, Mrs. Jepp," Ross said as Mary caught up with them.

"Yes I do," she said. "I found her. It is a her?" Ross looked at Mary for a moment.

"Yes," he said, "it is a her." Mary nodded.

"I thought so," she said. "From the hand. You see the nails were varnished, clear, but varnished." Ross nodded and the three of them fell into step, walking one behind the other, Indian-style, up the overgrown drive.

The Jepps stood beside the grave, looking down. They held hands. Ross watched them. After a moment Sam Jepp said, "Ellis Martin." Mary Jepp nodded in agreement and then the three of them turned and walked single file back to the edge of the field.

As they came out of Tinker Wood they were set upon by the television crew and by a journalist whom Ross particularly disliked. He told them that there was no comment, that he had nothing to say, and that when he did have something to say he would make a statement. He ushered the Jepps to the police car that would drive them home. Mary Jepp got to the car first and as she did she stopped to talk to the same young man Ross had seen them with earlier. As Ross came up he heard Mary Jepp say, "Yes, Ellis."

The man looked at her for a moment and then he turned and walked away across the field toward the farmhouse that Ross had only just noticed. The Jepps stood looking after him.

"Did he know her?" Ross asked. What was the

point in telling them that they shouldn't have said anything? Everyone would know soon enough that Ellis Martin was dead, whoever Ellis Martin was.

"Oh yes," Sam Jepp said. He was still watching the man as he climbed the stile and strode away across the next field toward the house.

"David Grainger," Mary Jepp said, in answer to the question that Ross had not asked. "This is his farm. His land borders ours," she added.

"And he knew Ellis Martin as well, did he?" asked Ross. The Jepps answered at once.

Sam Jepp simply said "Yes," but there was something in the way he said it that made Ross glance at him in time to catch the shadow on his face as he watched the rapidly receding David Grainger.

Mary Jepp said, "Everybody knew Ellis."

Then they got into the police car and Ross stood and watched as they were driven away.

David Grainger closed the front door behind him and leaned against it. For a moment he thought he might faint. He couldn't seem to catch his breath and his stomach was heaving. It was probably a good thing that he hadn't yet had any breakfast. He could still see Mary's face, her eyes full of concern. And that other man, that policeman in the dark overcoat whom he had sensed rather than actually seen. All that he had been able to think, all that he had wanted to do was to get home, to get here, safe inside the house, and away from all of those people.

He took a few steps up the hall and sat down heavily on the bottom step of the staircase. Put your head between your knees—wasn't that what they always said? But that wasn't what David wanted to do, not just now. Instead he reached for the phone and, pulling it over onto the stair beside him, he lifted the receiver. His fingers felt dull and heavy, as if they were made of putty, but despite that he managed to dial the number.

Kate Davidson was asleep. She was having a very pleasant dream, something to do with a garden and a summer afternoon. She was quite annoyed when she was jerked awake by the ringing of the telephone. She managed to glance at her watch on the bedside table before picking up the receiver. It was 7:45 in the morning. Kate hadn't been awake before half past eight for as long as she could remember. She did assume that there was a world that went on before then, but she had no desire at all to be a part of it. She thought of saying something rude and anatomically specific into the telephone as she answered but gave up the idea. It might be a dealer or a demented and fabulously wealthy patron of the arts who wanted to buy her work for a demented and fabulously inflated price. You never knew. It was, however, neither a dealer nor a patron of the arts. It was David Grainger sounding very odd.

"David?" she said, sitting up in bed. "What's the matter?"

"They've found Ellis." David's voice was harsh and he seemed to be out of breath.

"What?" Kate asked. "What are you talking about?"

"They've found her, buried in Tinker Wood."

Kate said nothing. Her brain didn't seem to be functioning properly.

"Kate?" David sounded on the verge of panic.

She shook her head, trying to clear her mind, to

hear the words correctly. Kate was already climbing out of bed, the receiver still in her hand. "David," she said. "David, hang on. I'll be right there."

Ross had given permission for the body to be taken away. It would, he thought, give the ghouls some pictures for their evening news. He knew that he wasn't being fair. Just like him, they were only doing their job.

He stood at the edge of the field and made a statement. There was very little that he could tell them at this time, but he answered a few questions nonetheless. The body had been discovered yesterday afternoon. He could not release an identity until relatives had been notified. No, they didn't know how long she had been dead. Yes, they could confirm that it was a female and that there was good reason to believe that she had been unlawfully killed by a person or persons unknown. The police were treating it as murder.

As he began walking away the journalists and onlookers turned away from him and closed in on the police ambulance. The black plastic body bag slid gently in on a stretcher, its chrome zips glinting in the morning sunlight. Ross looked back as he reached his car. The ambulance was pulling out. The television crew, satisfied for now, were closing up shop, rushing to get back to start their editing. Even Ross's least favorite journalist seemed to have gone off to the pub to phone in his copy. Now only the police and a few of the villagers were left. It was just after 8:00 A.M.

Ross was getting into his car when something across the field caught his eye. A flash of red moved up the driveway of the farm opposite and stopped in front of

David Grainger's house. As Ross watched, a figure got out of the car, ran across the courtyard, and went into the house. Ross thought that it was a woman, but he couldn't be sure from this distance. Whoever it was they had been in a hurry. It was early for David Grainger to be having visitors. And this was hardly a farmhand or the daily help. In Ross's experience they rarely drove red Porsches.

Chapter

2.

The local police station was in Millbrook, a few miles from Wildesham and May Green, and it was there that Ross set up his headquarters. He had been given an office for his personal use. It was a small, square box with a simulated oak desk and two simulated oak chairs. There was a large window that looked onto the station car park and the main street of the tiny market town beyond.

Ross, who had once been regarded as a rising star within the upper echelons of London's Metropolitan Police, was now on loan to the Kent County C.I.D. as a senior homicide investigator. The Met considered the loan temporary, a gentle humoring of a prima donna undergoing a momentary setback. Ross considered it permanent, refusing to see the death of his wife as a "glitch" in his career. He had fled the fast track and was happy where he was. The Met was confident that, given time, he would change his mind. Ross was equally confident that he would not.

Now the resources of the Millbrook station, which consisted of six telephones, two typewriters, and a Xerox machine, were at Ross's disposal. In addition, he was fully backed by the rather more considerable facilities of the County C.I.D. They had suggested moving a mobile unit into the station car park, but Ross had vetoed the idea. He did not need caravans, computer lists, and squadrons of clever young men to intimidate the locals. What he did need was the arrival of Detective Inspector Davies.

Ross had drafted Owen Davies on special request from the Met. Davies was a small, sly Welshman with a Celtic smile, a glare to match, and a peculiar ability to upset people. He was likely to ask indelicate questions at the wrong time, pinch reports before they were released, and ignore calls on his car radio that he considered to be a waste of time. At one time or another Ross had found all of these dubious attributes useful. Owen was a busybody and a sneak and that alone made him perfectly qualified, in Ross's eyes, to handle the day-to-day running of an investigation. Owen made it his business to know what everyone else knew and to find out what they were doing about it. He also made it his business to make sure that the information was passed on to Ross. Owen was fiercely loyal. He sometimes tugged his forelock and called Ross "Master," but insolent though he was, Ross knew that Owen was made of rock. He was a good man to trust your life to, should that unfortunate necessity arise.

Now Ross sat in his boxy little office and stared out of the window and waited for Owen to arrive with the first progress reports. The main purpose of Owen was that he left Ross free to think. In this case, as in all other cases, Ross began by making a list of the facts. It was not that Chief Inspector Ross didn't trust his instincts, but he had learned to be wary of them at first glance, or rather first twinge. Instincts and facts had to run in tandem. It was like music or painting. The facts were the rhythms, the notes, the colors, the draftsmanship beneath the perfect portrait. The instinct was the inspiration, the soul, the part of the picture that turned it from depiction into reality. You had to hang the instinct on the framework of facts, building layer by layer until the whole became real and inevitable.

Ross was pleased with this little analogy. He was less pleased with his list of facts. So far there was little that he could say about the circumstances of the death of Ellis Martin. He pulled out another piece of paper from the plywood desk drawer and began to compile another list. This was an instinct list. Later he would match the two lists, pairing his feelings with the facts before him. Ross believed firmly that one had feelings about things for a reason. If the reason was wrong then the feeling might well be irrelevant and therefore would have to be crossed out. But if the facts of the matter fit the feeling, well, that was a different story.

The first thing that Ross wrote on the top of his instinct list was a name and that name was "David Grainger." There was a great deal that Chief Inspector Ross thought that he would like to know about David Grainger. Before he could add anything else to the list there was a knock on the door. Ross didn't bother to shout "Come in." He knew it was Owen and that Owen came in whether you wanted him to or not. Ross was convinced that Owen would be a very good policeman one day, if one of his colleagues didn't kill him first.

Owen sat down on the other simulated oak chair and put the folder that he had been carrying on Ross's desk.

Ross looked at it for a moment. "Well," Ross asked, "what does it say?"

Owen smiled, then got up and took off his overcoat. It was a rather nice overcoat, Ross noted, a loden green shooting coat, probably bought by Owen's wife, Miranda. Owen hung the coat up carefully on a hanger.

"It doesn't say much," he said, turning around, "and that, Master, is a fact."

"Go on," said Ross.

"Well," Owen continued, "it's a strange thing. Forensics are coming up very dry. Of course we'll have the identity confirmed through her dental records, but there's no real doubt as to who she is. As for the rest, they've only been at it a few hours, but even so. No bits of material stuck on brambles, no sign of a struggle, nothing in that old cottage either. Of course there's not a hope of a footprint or a tire track, not after that storm last week. Whoever our man is, or woman, for that matter, they've been very lucky. They have also, however, been very careful."

"Planned," Ross said, looking out of the window. It was not a question.

"Very carefully planned, I should say," said Owen. "It all adds up. With the exception of the video card and a few tissues, there was virtually nothing in her pockets or on her person. No keys, no purse, nothing. Of course, they could have been stolen."

"Not very likely," said Ross.

"No, I don't think so either," Owen replied.

"So," said Ross, still looking out of the window,

"either Ellis Martin was murdered somewhere else and the body was taken to the spot and buried, or—" He let Owen finish the sentence.

"Or she went there of her own accord to meet someone she knew. Or she was out for a walk and someone jumped her, murdered her, and buried the body."

"Do you find that likely, by the way?" Ross asked.

"No," said Owen, "I don't. It's possible, of course. But for a start, she doesn't appear to have been raped and, secondly, I don't tend toward random killer theories."

"No," said Ross. "On the whole, people get murdered for a reason. It may not be a good reason, but there usually is one. Even Charles Manson had a reason." He swung around in his chair and faced Owen. "What else?"

"Well, I told them to keep looking and to look harder. After that there's the preliminary medical report. She was killed, it appears, by a single blow to the head with a heavy, edged instrument."

"Something like a spade?"

"Exactly."

"From in front or behind?"

"From behind and slightly to the left. The killer could have been right- or left-handed, man or a woman, provided that they had reasonable strength in their arms and shoulders."

"Nothing very helpful there. Go on."

"She probably wouldn't have seen the attacker, but she might have seen the weapon the moment before it hit her. She has been dead for no more than a week. There are no obvious signs of a struggle and, as I said before, there is no reason at this point in time to believe that she was sexually assaulted. All of this will be confirmed, of course."

"Of course," said Ross. "And in the meantime?"

Owen put the report back on the desk. "In the meantime," he said, "I've told them to keep at it double-time in the woods. I've started them on house to house statements and I have the keys to Ellis Martin's house from her daily, Mrs. Jeffers, who is actually a biweekly. I've put a constable on duty up there. I thought you'd want to be the first one in."

Ross stood. "Let's go and have a look. Did you get a statement from Mrs. Jeffers?"

"Yes," said Owen, as the two men put on their coats. "I did. It's as unhelpful as everything else about this case. She came in to clean last Wednesday, as usual. She comes on Mondays and Wednesdays. Miss Martin wasn't there, but apparently there's nothing unusual in that. Miss Martin, it seems, is often away. She has a fiancé in London—"

Ross stopped buttoning his coat and looked at him.

"All right," Owen said, grinning, "So it wasn't as unhelpful as all that. And yes, we are trying to locate the fiancé now."

"Tell me as we go," Ross said, and he led the way out of the station to Owen's car.

They turned out of the police station and down through the main street of Millbrook. Ellis's house was in Wildesham, a ten minute drive away.

They drove up the hill toward the church and turned into a side lane before Owen continued. "In any case," he said, "Mrs. Jeffers presumed that Ellis was away. She doesn't open the cupboards, so she wouldn't have known about whether or not her toilet things and other personal bits and pieces were missing. She didn't see Ellis last Wednesday, nor the previous Monday, the seventh. The last time that she did see her was on Wednesday, February second. She says that, as far as she can remember, everything seemed perfectly normal."

"And so far that's it?"

Owen nodded as he turned into another lane signposted for Widlesham. "So far that's it," he said.

Ellis Martin's house stood on the far side of the village quite a way back from the road. The drive was fronted by a pair of white gates. A police constable was standing outside. The constable came over to the car window, spoke briefly with Owen, and opened the gates.

Ross's first thought was that it was a very pretty house. It was not particularly impressive, as such, but it was by no means insubstantial. The house was built of warm red brick and red Kentish tile. The front door and the woodwork had been painted the traditional white. The garden was well kept and ringed by a tall, clipped hedge. At the bottom of the lawn a small gate led through an archway into woodland beyond. There was a garage to one side whose doors were closed. Police tape made a bright orange line across the front of them. It was the only jarring note in an otherwise peaceful scene.

The house was bigger than Ross had expected. It didn't seem like the sort of house that women as young as Ellis Martin usually owned.

"It was left to her by an aunt about five years ago," Owen said, reading his mind. "Apparently her only relative. Ellis's parents died when she was young, left her a trust and a numbered account." They began to walk up the neatly graveled path.

"How old was she?" Ross asked.

"Twenty-nine," Owen replied. "She would have been thirty in June."

Ross stopped and looked up at the house. Suddenly life seemed quite rotten to him, despite the bright, unseasonable sunshine. A young, beautiful woman, a woman who should have had everything ahead of her, had simply been rubbed out. He was here only to poke and pry and invade the corners of her life. With luck his prying would lead him to the person who had taken it upon themselves to terminate her existence but, in the end, what good would that do? The damage had already been done. It had been done not more than a week ago not half a mile from where he stood and what could he have done about it? A week ago he hadn't even known her name. It is my job in this life, he thought, always to arrive on the scene one moment too late.

Owen was already at the front door.

"I don't want anyone in here," Ross said from the path. "No one except forensics. Put somebody on it, twenty-four hours." Owen smiled and before he could reach out to lift the knocker, Constable Glen opened the door.

"I've taken care of it," Owen said and together the two men stepped into the front hall.

That Ellis Martin had been possessed of what is conventionally known as good taste was obvious. The house was pleasantly and expensively decorated. No frills and ruffles, nothing overdone and nothing too new. Nothing very personal either, thought Ross, at least not on the ground floor. In fact the only sign of habitation that he could see at all were two pairs of very clean, green wellington boots which were lined up on the mat inside the kitchen door. Above them a gray cardigan hung on a coat peg and beside that there was a bulletin board which held only an out-of-date flyer announcing some kind of meeting to protest area planning policy.

The kitchen was large and bright with blue and white tiles and a matching blue Aga. Beyond it there was a downstairs cloakroom, a dining room with French windows, and two sitting rooms. The entire house appeared to be spotless.

"The damned woman's cleaned, hasn't she, in the last week?"

Owen nodded. "I'm afraid so; twice."

So much for anything, thought Ross. She's probably the thorough type as well. "Do you think that it's something our killer counted on? That the house would be cleaned? Do you think it's something they knew?"

"They could have done," said Owen, "if they were local, or knew Ellis well."

"Which they may well have done," said Ross. "I know, I know," he added. "Ninety-five percent or some such thing of all murders are perpetrated by someone the victim knew well."

"Well, they'd have to be, wouldn't they?" said Owen. "You really have to get under someone's skin to get them to murder you."

Ross stood in the sitting room looking at a portrait that hung over the fireplace. The style was distinctive, romantic without sacrificing any power. If Ross was right it was close to being a museum quality piece.

The subject was a woman in her forties. Ross assumed that it was the aunt. Perhaps, he thought, this is what Ellis would have looked like in fifteen years. Now she had been denied the chance to grow old and eternal youth was hers. Not much of a bargain. Ross peered at the portrait looking for a signature. A little mental shake of congratulation. He was right; it was a DeLaslo.

"Who inherits?" he asked, turning back to Owen.

"We don't know yet," Owen said, "we're trying to find out. I haven't touched a thing. I thought you'd want to go through the desk yourself. It's upstairs."

Ross nodded. They'd only found her some twenty hours ago. It was early days yet, he told himself as he climbed the stairs. "Why do I feel that this case is unlucky?" he asked Owen from the top of the stairway.

Owen looked up at him and winked. "Because you haven't had any luck yet," he said. Sometimes Ross hated Welshmen.

The upstairs looked more promising. There were three bedrooms. Two were obviously guestrooms. The third must have been Ellis's room. It was a large room done in yellow with a large and immaculate en-suite bathroom. Ross went through the dressing table drawers while Owen took the bathroom cabinets.

"No sleeping tablets, no tranquilizers, no birth control pills, no diaphragm. She wasn't neurotic, slept soundly, and was a nun. Unless she had a coil or a cervical cap. Or he used sheaths. Or she left her diaphragm in his safekeeping, like a modern chastity belt." Owen delivered this monologue from the bathroom doorway.

"Thank you," said Ross, "that's fascinating."

The dressing table drawers were models of cleanliness and order. Handkerchiefs were folded neatly in one little pile. Next to them were three lipsticks. In the next drawer there was a Mason and Pearson hairbrush and nothing else. The hairs in it, he knew, would all turn out to be Ellis's. Owen was clearly having no greater success with the bureau drawers or the wardrobe. Where in Hell did the woman keep her life, Ross thought angrily. It had to be somewhere. He slammed the drawer shut and went looking for the desk.

The next room along the corridor was obviously the room that Ellis used as her study. He paused for a moment in the doorway, surprised at the excitement he felt. There, sitting on a small armchair, was what had to be Ellis Martin's handbag.

It was an expensive, black Gucci bag with a gold clasp. Ross put his gloves on before he picked it up and emptied it very carefully. Luckily the bag wasn't too new. Older handbags were always more revealing. They'd had more time to collect receipts, bits of paper, old envelopes, all the tiny paraphernalia that went into making up a life. This bag had its fair share of all those things, along with two shiny black lipsticks with the distinctive Chanel mark on top, a compact face powder, and a fountain pen that looked as though it was expensive. But, more importantly, there were four other items that Ross had been looking for. There was a wallet, a check book, an address book, and a diary.

Owen had followed Ross into the room and stood watching. Ross opened the wallet carefully. Inside there was one hundred and fifty pounds in cash and all of the usual credit cards.

"She was not murdered for money," said Ross. He

nodded at the desk. Owen opened it carefully and went quickly through the cubbyholes.

"She gave to Greenpeace and Save The Children," he said. In the little central drawer he found a set of car keys and a date book.

Ross was thumbing through the date book. Years of practice enabled him to turn the thin watered pages almost without touching them. In his experience people came in two categories as far as date books were concerned. They either wrote everything down or they only made the most obscure and unhelpful mess of personal hieroglyphics. Some personal calendars were so arcane that they made breaking the Enigma code look easy. But it looked like Ellis Martin was one of the ones who wrote everything down. Ross felt his luck beginning to change. There, for instance, under Friday, February fourth, were the words, "Kate, P.M." And on Saturday, February fifth, there was "Canterbury, A.M." and this was followed by a line with an arrow that went all the way through the following week and stopped at February twelfth, under which was written "return Wildesham."

"She was planning to come home today," Ross said. Owen looked up from the desk.

"What?"

"Canterbury," said Ross. "She seems to have been going to go to Canterbury for a week."

Owen looked into the desk for a moment and then reached into one of the cubbys and pulled something out. It was a brochure and he read the cover title out loud.

"Documentary in Production. A Special Seminar of The British Film Institute. Hosted by The Department of Film, University of Kent, Canterbury." Owen flipped open the page. "It was a residential seminar.

Ran from the fifth to the twelfth. The application form on the back's been clipped out."

"Bring it with you," said Ross. He gathered up the contents of the handbag and started for the stairs. "And Owen," he said over his shoulder, "get forensics in here right away. I want them to go over this place like there's no tomorrow."

Owen hurried down the stairs after Ross. He paused just long enough to speak to Constable Glen, who had retired discreetly to the garden while they had been in the house.

"Nobody's to get in and nobody's to breathe until forensics gets here, right?" Owen said. "Not even you, old boy," he added. "Sorry, you'll have to wait outside." Glen nodded and then Owen was gone, racing down the path after Chief Inspector Ross.

Barry Glen stood on the front steps of the house and watched them get into the car and drive out through the front gates. They don't half make a funny pair, he thought. The Chief Inspector was a great tall fellow in a dark overcoat. He was the kind that looked a bit as if he had no real muscles holding all his bones together, as if he were just a bunch of awkward angles in an expensive suit. The other chap was small and built like a boxer with that funny green coat with the pleat down the back. They were odd looking, no question about it. Still, thought Barry Glen, puffing his chest out, it was the best thing that had happened around here since he joined the force. This was why he'd become a policeman. Here he was guarding material evidence in a murder case that would most likely be on the BBC news tonight. And if not that, definitely Southern Region. Angie was going to be dead impressed, all right.

Chapter
3
•

Where to?" Owen asked as they turned out of the gates. Ross did not seem to be listening. He was looking through the date book, scanning the pages from January first. Owen stopped the car and asked once more, "Where to?"

Ross looked up for a second and then returned his attention to the date book. Instead of answering Owen's question he said, "The car in the garage of the Martin house?"

"A white BMW 535, registered to Ellis Martin."

"Locked," said Ross. "No sign of a struggle? No sign of having been moved? No sign of anything out of the ordinary?"

"That's right," Owen said. "The same with the garage, the garden and the garden shed."

"Back to the station, please," said Ross. "Forensics won't find anything," he added. The thought seemed to satisfy him. Owen thought he looked quite smug.

Later, after finishing some rather nasty sandwiches

and some even nastier coffee, Owen was dispatched to find out about the film seminar and to check on how house-to-house statements were coming. Ross studied the date book. Occasionally he would cross-reference it to the address book. After a half an hour of this he began a list of names. He had just written the third name when Owen returned. Without looking up Ross said, "The boyfriend, or fiancé or whatever—"

"Significant other. They call them significant others these days," Owen said.

"Well, whatever. Go and talk to him." Ross was printing carefully onto his list, like a child in a school spelling quiz.

"That would mean going to Spain," said Owen.

"What?" Ross stopped printing and finally looked up. Now at least Owen had his attention.

"Spain," he said. "That's where he is. He's been there since the first. At a film festival. He works for the British Film Institute. He gets back tomorrow," Owen added as he sat down.

"Ah," said Ross. "Hence our young lady's interest in film. Documentary in Production, wasn't it?"

"That's right," said Owen, "and I'll tell you something about that as well. She never got there."

"Ask me if I'm surprised," said Ross.

"There's more," Owen went on. "On Saturday morning, the morning that the seminar started, the office of the film department at Canterbury got a message. Apparently someone rang to say that Ellis Martin had to cancel because of ill health."

"What?"

"That's right," said Owen. "She was all registered and paid up. Some of the students arrived on the Friday night, but they didn't have to be there until about eleven on the Saturday. Some time that morning someone called the office and told them that Ellis Martin was ill, that she wouldn't be attending."

"Someone called them or Ellis Martin called them?"

"We don't really know. The girl who took the message was only working there as a temp during the seminar. Apparently her job finished and she left last night. We're trying to find her. The girl who runs the office said that she assumed that the person who rang wasn't Ellis Martin herself because she remembers something about the wording of the message, which said that 'Ellis Martin was ill and wouldn't be attending.' She also got the impression that it wasn't Ellis Martin herself because when she asked the office temp if she'd explained about the percentage of the tuition refund that students could get with a certified doctor's excuse, the temp said that, 'yes, she'd started to, but that the person on the other end had put the phone down and that she'd thought that was particularly odd.'"

Ross made a long whistling sound.

"There's more," said Owen.

"More from the film school?"

Owen shook his head. "No, sorry. We're working on that as hard as we can. On unearthing the temp, I mean. No, there's more about Ellis Martin's movements in the weeks before February fifth, from the house-to-house statements. It seems that she was seen around and about, you know, the shop, the newsagent, that sort of thing, up to about noon on Friday, February fourth. Apparently she went into the local shop at just about noon on the fourth to buy some milk. The owner's wife remembers it because they close at noon on Friday for half a day and Ellis only just made it in. After that there's nothing, at least not that we can turn up."

Ross looked down at his carefully printed list. "I think," he said, "that it's time that we called on Kate."

"Kate?" asked Owen.

Ross pushed the date book back across the desk to where Owen could see it.

"February fourth," Owen read. "Kate. Who is she?" Ross was already standing up and reaching for his overcoat.

"There's only one Kate in Miss Martin's address book," he said. "She's Kate Davidson. She lives in Wildesham in a house called The Hall."

"The Hall" was what estate agents like to refer to as "a house of substance," which meant, thought Ross, that it was big. It was a mile or so outside of Wildesham on top of a hill. It was a large brick Georgian house and in the mild afternoon sunshine it appeared to be slightly tinged with gold. It was a wealthy man's house. Or, in this case, a wealthy woman's.

There was no response when they knocked on the large white front door. There was nothing as vulgar as a bell.

"Perhaps they don't have unexpected visitors here," said Owen as they stepped away from the door. "Perhaps they only have invited guests. In which case we'd better find the servants' and tradesmen's entrance."

"Yes," said Ross, "perhaps we had."

The courtyard where Owen had parked was empty.

Perhaps no one was at home. More likely, this was the sort of house that had a back drive for those who were *au fait,* a back drive and banks of garages in a converted stable block tucked away out of sight.

Owen found the kitchen door at the side of the house. Coming around the corner to join him, Ross felt a jolt of surprise and pleasure at what awaited him there. Owen stood in the middle of what could only be described as a proper, old-fashioned herb garden. The stone path had been divided into a network of diamonds at the side of the house and each diamond-shaped bed was a different herb, or would be when spring came. Tiny brass plaques set into the brick announced what each bed would become. Ross leaned down to read the familiar names, "marjoram," "thyme," "chervil," "basil." They were all there. The plaques had recently been polished. This house might not welcome unexpected visitors but it was kept by someone who still knew that thyme and sage came out of the ground and were not harvested from trees in little glass bottles.

Ross looked up and saw Owen watching him.

"I should think she'll be an old battle-ax in tweeds and twin sets from the look of that lot," Owen said. "Not that it matters much either way." He had stepped back from the door and was looking up at the house. "Because either she's out or she's not answering."

"Let's try the back," said Ross. He was reluctant to give up quite so easily. Besides, he admitted to himself, he wanted to see the rest of the garden.

He led the way along the brick pavement that surrounded the house. He felt Owen behind him, dragging by a pace or two like a sulky child, no doubt thinking that it would be a far more efficient use of time to send a constable to wait until the elusive Kate Davidson returned. He was probably right, but Ross didn't really care. He could feel stubbornness rising up in him and he lengthened his stride slightly, well aware that this would make Owen have to hurry, annoying him further.

Behind the house the brick opened into a patio fronted by an entire wall of French windows. The lawn fell away down a slight hill toward a pond at the bottom of the rise. Ross paused, feeling slightly silly. He had come charging around the back with great decisive steps and now he had no idea of where to go. What did he think he was going to do, press his nose against the windows in the hope of catching this woman hiding inside? He was just wondering how he could recover his dignity when he heard a voice say, "Is it me you're looking for?"

The woman walking across the lawn toward him was not a battle-ax nor was she wearing tweeds. In fact, she was wearing a pair of black trousers and a black sweater. She had long, red, very curly hair that was fastened up on top of her head in such a way as to make her look slightly like a tall, black, walking dishmop. She was much younger than Ross had expected.

"I'm sorry to disturb you," he said. "We're looking for a Mrs. Davidson. A Katherine Davidson."

She smiled at him and put out her hand.

"I'm not disturbed," she said, shaking his hand with a firm schoolgirl grasp. "I look like this all the time. Mrs. Davidson is my mother, but her name is

Elaine. She lives in America and she hasn't seen Ellis Martin in years. I do take it that you are the police and that it is Ellis that you're here to talk about?"

"That's right," Ross said.

"Well, it's me you're looking for," she said. "I'm Kate Davidson."

"I'm Chief Inspector Ross," said Ross, "and this is Detective Inspector Davies."

"I should think you'd better come in," she said as she shook Owen's hand. They followed her obediently through one of the French windows.

Ross watched her as she made coffee. What did she remind him of? She had the long rangy figure of a natural athlete. A swimmer perhaps? No, not quite. There was rather more to her than that. You could almost see her brain turning over, wheels clicking and turning under that mop of hair. She's nervous, he thought, but I'm not sure it's because of us. She may be someone who's always like this, a restless, driven, energetic soul. Very sure of herself. A rather frightening woman, to some minds. Perhaps one who trades on that slightly? He wasn't quite certain. What on earth does she do down here? he wondered.

She answered the question for him.

"I'm sorry you couldn't find me," she said as she poured the coffee. "I was rather expecting you. I should have been up here but I was down at the studio. I'm a painter," she added as she put the coffeepot down. She glanced over her shoulder at Ross to see how he'd taken this piece of information. "Don't worry," she said, "I'm not particularly famous. You needn't have heard of me."

Ross noticed the use of the word "particularly." So, she's famous enough, he thought. She wants me to know that she's not a country girl who dabbles in watercolor. She could have been an actress, he thought, looking at her. She's got that kind of charisma. And just now, Ross said to himself, it's all being marshaled into a very interesting performance for me.

Kate had debated aloud with herself as to whether or not they should go into the living room, as she called it. She came to the conclusion that they should stay in the kitchen, if Owen and Ross could stand it. They both thought that they could and now the three of them were seated at the kitchen table.

"So," said Kate, getting up again almost as soon as she had sat down, "what can I do for you?" She took an ashtray out of the cupboard and lit a cigarette. "I know, they're awful," she said. "But we all have our vices." She blew the match out and placed it in the ashtray and then she looked at Ross. The mask, whatever it had been, had fallen away and her unmade-up face was sober and intelligent. The performance might not be over, but at least she was giving him her full attention.

"Ellis Martin," Ross said. "In her diary she made a note to the effect that she was going to see you, I think. On the evening of Friday, February fourth."

Kate nodded. "That's right," she said, "but she didn't."

"How's that, Miss?" It was Owen speaking. Kate turned to him.

"She was supposed to come here for a drink that Friday evening. She never appeared."

"You're quite sure? You couldn't have been in your studio? Not heard her arrive?"

Kate put out the cigarette. "Like this afternoon, you mean? No," she shook her head. "I was expecting her.

I was here in the house doing something or other. You know, reading, pottering. Ellis never showed up."

"And what did you do when she didn't show up?" Ross asked.

"Nothing," said Kate.

"Nothing?" asked Owen.

Kate shrugged. "I carried on with whatever I was doing. I made myself some supper. I probably watched television. I went to bed. No Ellis."

"Isn't that a little odd?" asked Owen.

"Her not coming or me watching television?" Kate smiled.

"I was thinking," said Owen, "of your not getting worried. Not trying to contact her. After all, if you've invited someone to your house for a drink and they simply don't appear, wouldn't it be natural to telephone? To wonder where they'd got to? To be concerned?"

"Of course it would," said Kate. "If you've invited someone to your house for a drink. And I might have, probably would have done all of those things, had I invited Ellis here. But I hadn't. Ellis invited Ellis here. And frankly, when she didn't show up I assumed she'd forgotten, or thought of something better to do, and I considered myself fortunate to have made a lucky escape."

"Oh," said Ross.

She looked at him for a moment and seemed to be trying to make up her mind about something. Then she stood up and walked across the room.

"Look, Inspector," she said, "I'm very sorry that Ellis is dead. But you might as well hear this from me, since I'm sure you'll hear it anyway. I didn't like Ellis Martin. I really didn't like her very much at all. So when she invited herself up here I was, to be honest, rather relieved when she didn't show up and I didn't have to put up with her. It was the sort of thing Ellis did, anyway, not showing up at places. I really didn't think anything of it. If I'd known that she was going to end up whacked on the head or whatever it was, up in Tinker Wood, I would have been more concerned when she didn't appear. But as it was, I'm afraid that I didn't give it a second thought."

"Then you weren't friends—you and Ellis Martin?" asked Owen. Kate paused for a moment.

"Yes we were," she said. "We were once very good friends. But that was a long time ago." She looked out of the window and Ross thought that he saw something like sadness or regret move across her face. Whatever it was, it vanished when she turned back to them.

"We grew up together," she said, "in the summers, anyway. I'm an American, in case you hadn't guessed. This is my parents' house. When I was a child we came here every summer. Me, my parents, and my brother. Ellis came here to her aunt's. Her parents had been killed, oh, I don't know, when she was very little and her aunt, Jane Martin, was her guardian. Actually, I think she finally adopted Ellis. In any case, we all came here for the summers and at Christmas as well. We did Pony Club together and all that sort of thing. From the time we were about seven, Ellis and I were inseparable. I suppose that she was my 'best friend.' You know how little girls are."

"And later," asked Ross, "what happened?"

Kate shrugged. "We became teenagers. I went to school in the States, Ellis here. We still saw each other in the summers. We went to University. Again, me there, her here, and that was when we fell out of touch. I suppose we outgrew each other. We didn't see each other for years and years and when we did, well, we just found that we didn't like each other very much. You know how it is. Of course we both lived here, on and off. It wasn't as if we hissed at each other in the street or anything," Kate added, smiling. "We just weren't close anymore, that's all."

"I see," said Ross, standing up.

"Thank you for your time," said Owen, following his example.

"Just one more thing," asked Ross. "Before the non-event of Friday the fourth, when was the last time you saw her or heard from her?"

Kate thought for a moment. "A few days before," she said. "Maybe on the Monday or Tuesday. I saw her in the village. That was when she asked me if I'd be home on Friday evening and if she could stop by."

"She didn't say why? Didn't mention that she wanted to speak to you about something specific?"

Kate shook her head. "No."

"And that didn't strike you as strange? Given that the two of you were no longer very friendly?"

"It may have done," said Kate.

"I see," said Ross. "Well, don't let us keep you from your studio."

Kate smiled. "I won't," she said. "Here, let me show you out the front."

They followed her through the kitchen and into the front hall. She shook hands with each of them again as they stood on the front steps.

"We may want to speak to you again, Miss Davidson," said Ross.

"If I'm not here, I'm in my studio," she said. And

then, as he reached the bottom of the steps, she spoke again. "Inspector?" He looked up and paused. She stood above him, frowning. "That's why it's important, isn't it? That Ellis didn't show up? She was already dead, wasn't she?" Ross looked at her for a moment.

"I don't know," he said. She nodded at him and then he turned and walked away to the waiting car.

Chapter
4
·

It was just over twenty-four hours since Mary Jepp had discovered the body of Ellis Martin and yet it seemed to Ross much longer. It's always like that in the beginning, thought Ross. It's because all of the information comes tumbling in at once, if you're lucky. Forensics, pathology, material evidence arrive in a quick energetic slew, a tide of puzzle pieces spilled out in front of you. One was inevitably exhausted, dog-tired with the sheer physical work of the thing. It wasn't until later, until the time when all of the so-called facts were in, that you were able to slow down long enough to let your mind go to work and try to tell you what it all meant. It was then that you could begin to try to understand how and why it was that someone had got themselves into the position of being bashed on the head, shot, strangled, eliminated by another of their fellow men.

It was exactly the same, really, as a good newspaper story. Who, what, when, where, and why, the bywords

of every worthwhile reporter. It was really ju[...]
same for the police, thought Ross, except th[...]
police work one ingredient always stood out. Give me
the "why" and nine and one-half times out of ten, I
can tell you who and then how.

Now, at home in his sitting room with the files and
reports spread out around him, Ross wondered why it
was that Ellis Martin had come to be buried in Tinker
Wood. He stood up, stretching out his long, crane-like
legs. His "at home" corduroy trousers were getting
slightly thin and furry around the knees and cuffs. He
could feel the hint of a draft in the seat of his pants
that meant that they were afflicted there as well. He
looked down at them sadly. They had been through a
good many weekends, these trousers, and soon he
would have to relinquish them to Mrs. Stubbs, his
daily, who would cut them into neat triangles and use
them for polishing the sideboard. I'm growing too
fond of things, thought Ross. It must be because I'm
getting older. He knew that it was also because it
would mean another trip to London, another day
spent in the familiar male environs of Swaine, Adney,
Brigg and Lobbs and Huntsman where he would be
re-equipped with trousers and shirts and strong brown
leather shoes to see him through another five years of
weekend gardening and fishing.

Even after three years he still didn't like going back
to London. Kendal was everywhere. She was his
ghost-girl. He saw her on street corners, still looked for
her in crowds. He could be reduced to confused
silence by the familiar movement of a woman's hand,
a voice in a restaurant, hair that was a certain shade of
blond. Kendal had loved the city. On foot she had
discovered its churches, its gardens, and its secrets.

And of course she had also known its shops. With great joy and good taste, Kendal spent freely of his money and her own. After her death Ross thought that the salesman in Kent and Curwin and the lady behind the counter at Charbonnel and Walker had missed her almost as much as he did. That had been almost comforting as he had prowled the places that made up their life together, always thinking somehow that he had merely misplaced her, would find her waiting for him if he could only remember where.

Ross had known Kendal almost all of his life. He thought that he could remember quite clearly the first time that he had seen her. He was twelve and had come home from boarding school for the Easter vacation. His father had just been made a cabinet minister and to celebrate that fact a large garden party was held. Parents were encouraged to bring their offspring and equally encouraged to propel them toward the back of the house where there was an ample supply of non-alcoholic punch, blancmange shapes, and sandwiches with crusts. The Right Honorable Miss Kendal Leggat and her sisters wore matching hair ribbons and ate triangle-cut sandwiches whole. Later, at a boys-only game of cricket, they insisted on being allowed to play and Kendal hit an impressive six off of Ross. Eleven years later he married her.

In the twelve short years they were married, Ross never ceased to adore her, just as he had adored her that first afternoon so long ago in an English summer garden. As an adult, she was still petite, delicate, and tiny. She would link her arm through his, skipping to keep up with him and call him "my husband, the

Copper." Life had been great fun. Then Kendal was dead and everything was different.

Ross gave himself a little mental shake and went to change the disc on his CD player. He allowed himself the unusual indulgence of brooding and chose Brahms. He sternly told himself to think about Ellis Martin.

No need to read the files; he knew what was in them by heart. Forensics had turned up precisely nothing: no skin under the fingernails, no foreign hairs, no blood that was not her own, no material threads, no sign of a struggle. The storm the night before she was found and the wind on the preceding days had successfully eradicated any footprints that might have been found. There were no tire tracks on the old drive leading up to the cottage for the same reason. The weather had done its job well and now there was nothing to indicate that anyone had been there. Nothing, that was, except a dead girl with a gash in her head buried in a wood.

All of this merely confirmed Ross's initial instincts. Ellis Martin had not been killed by a wandering psychopath. People rarely were, despite what the tabloids said. And wandering maniacs were notoriously messy. Nor could this be described as a "crime of passion"; there was nothing spur of the moment about it. This was a murder that had been carefully planned and executed. Someone had thought long and hard about killing Ellis Martin, which meant that someone had a very good reason for wanting her dead.

Ross sat down again and closed his eyes. What do I know, he asked himself. You know that Ellis Martin was a twenty-nine-year-old woman with no criminal record. She was wealthy, in a moderate kind of way. She owned a nice house and a nice car and could afford to maintain them and herself without working. She was engaged to be married. She gave money to Save the Children and to Greenpeace and showed some interest in local planning issues. She was interested in film and possibly in other arts as well. She was a well-bred sort of a girl with what our mothers would have called "good taste," if a bit flashy.

She was last known to be seen alive in the village shop of the town that she lived in just before noon on Friday, February fourth. She was planning to go away for a week as of the next morning, but no bag was found to have been packed. Her housekeeper was quite certain that she hadn't started to get ready yet on the evidence that when the cupboards were opened they revealed that her facial things were untouched in the bathroom. Ellis Martin was, according to the good Mrs. Jeffers, the sort of girl who might be willing to abandon her earthly possessions but who would never go away for a week without her moisturizer.

So, Ellis had not begun to pack on Friday afternoon. Nor had she, on Friday evening, kept a date that she had made herself only a few days before. The next morning she had not arrived in Canterbury to attend a course for which she had paid four hundred pounds. Instead, someone had called the office of the school to say that Ellis was canceling due to illness. Someone who didn't want to speak on the phone any more than was necessary. Someone who was probably not Ellis but who knew that Ellis was dead.

And this, thought Ross, was interesting. Whomever this person was, they had known that Ellis was due to go to Canterbury for a week, something that even her own housekeeper had been unaware of. They had picked their timing carefully, giving themselves a week's grace before the alarm was raised that Ellis was missing.

At least a week, if not longer, thought Ross. Ellis could be assumed to have been in London or the country. And even when she was eventually reported missing, it could be a very long time indeed before anyone would think to look for her in Tinker Wood. It was merely bad luck on the murderer's part that Ellis was discovered as soon as she was. It was also bad luck that Ellis had noted in her date book that she was to meet Kate Davidson on the night of the fourth. Assuming that Kate Davidson was telling the truth, the fact that Ellis hadn't shown up at The Hall probably meant that she was already dead. Thanks to that little note in her date book and the good memory of the woman in the village shop, and provided that Kate wasn't lying, it was safe to assume that Ellis Martin had been killed some time between noon and the evening of the fourth. That fact alone was going to make his job much easier. As for the phone call to Canterbury, well, that was a risk that had to be taken. All that the killer could hope for, and quite reasonably so, was that enough time elapsed before Ellis was discovered that whomever took that call would become very hazy about the details and the voice. It was a reasonable thought on the whole. People who answer telephones in offices tend to forget the details of particular calls rather quickly.

Ellis Martin had neither been robbed nor assaulted. She was simply killed. What? Murder. When? Probably sometime between noon of February fourth and the evening of the same day. How? A single blow to the head with a heavy, edged instrument. Where? Either in Tinker Wood or in some other location that was probably not her own home. So, thought Ross, I am left with who and why, the inevitable terrible twins.

Ellis Martin's date book lay on the table beside him. He picked it up, running his thumb down the soft calfskin spine. It was the distinctive Asprey's purple and the small pen that fit into its side flap was lacquered the same color. Ross wondered if it had been a Christmas gift. Perhaps a stocking present from her fiancé? He had been through the book several times after it had been released from forensics. There was only one thing in it that puzzled him, that he could find no reference to in any of Ellis Martin's other papers, and that was the name "Clara Beale."

It had been written on the back flysheet of the little leather book in the clear finishing school hand that Ross had come to recognize as Ellis's. It was probably the name of a friend of a friend or a dressmaker or someone who arranged flowers for dinner parties. Clara Beale could be anyone and the chances were that her name meant nothing at all.

Still, Ross found loose ends disturbing and among the ones that disturbed him at the moment were the girl who had taken the telephone message at Canterbury and Ellis Martin's fiancé. They were doing everything they could to track down the office temp and Owen would be a Gatwick tomorrow to meet the man that Ellis had planned to marry. Poor sod, thought Ross. He would be looking for her as he came out of baggage collection, scanning the crowd with that slightly anxious look that people have before they pick out a familiar face. But for him there would be no familiar face. Instead he would be picked up and taken to the VIP room where a small Welsh policeman would try to break to him gently the fact that he would never see Ellis Martin again. What is the tactful way to tell a man that the woman he loves has been murdered, hit on the head and buried in a scrubby little wood?

The telephone rang, causing Ross to flinch in his chair before reaching out to answer it. He turned the music down as he heard Owen's voice.

"I hope I'm not disturbing you, Master," Owen said, "but I thought you'd want to know." Owen paused and Ross could see him smiling wickedly.

"Go on," Ross said.

"We've found the murder weapon." Owen presented his gift on a little silver platter of self-congratulation.

"Splendid," Ross said. "And?" Owen was a scrappy little terrier. He was eager to please and very capable, if not downright inspired. But he needed, metaphorically speaking, to have his tummy scratched from time to time. Not everyone understood this. Ross, however, was all too willing. The results were almost always worth the effort.

"A spade," Owen said. "Ordinary garden variety, pardon the pun. We found it down behind the cottage, to the side of the drive, under a bramble hedge. Wiped clean, but quickly. Given that, the protection from the undergrowth, and some luck, forensics will find their stuff."

"They won't find any fingerprints," said Ross.

"No, I wouldn't have thought so. Unless our chap's

a moron, and I think we can count that out. Oh," Owen added, "there's one more thing." He was saving the best for last. "It's branded."

"What?"

"You know, those marking things that can be burned in. It was all the rage a few years ago when equipment and tack was being pinched from farms down here and shipped by the lorry load over the channel. You could do it with rented kits or someone would come in and do it. Anyway, the spade handle's branded. With the initials 'W.P.'"

They spoke for a few moments longer before Owen said that he'd go straight to Gatwick in the morning. Ross wished him luck, sent his love to Miranda, and hung up. He turned the sound system up again and let the Brahms drift through the old house. He imagined the music rising like smoke, swirling up the brick chimney and out into the night, mingling with the wind that was rising, coming in from the sea across the North downs.

The initials "W.P." were familiar and yet he couldn't place them. He found the large-scale ordnance survey map of the area in one of the files and spread it out on the carpet. Sure enough, there it was. "W.P." would stand for Wildesham Place, one of the farms that bordered Tinker Wood. Ross felt a slight twinge of excitement, but it was best to check and be sure. He pulled out another of the files and sat back on his heels. Wildesham Place was owned by David Grainger.

By midnight it had begun to rain. The wind grew stronger and the bare trees that lined the drive up to The Hall made squeaking noises as they bent and rose and bent once more. The downstairs windows of The Hall were lit, and from the outside the warm electric light glowed through the curtains.

Inside Kate Davidson sat in the library. She liked the night. She often painted at night, especially in the summer when it seemed that it never got completely dark. In New England, where she had grown up, you could sometimes see the Northern lights on summer nights. As children they had sat on blankets on the lawn watching the explosions of milky green and yellow blossom out across the sky. But tonight it was very dark and Kate was not painting or thinking about her childhood. She had been sitting for some time in a large armchair beside the unlit fire. She was thinking about David Grainger and she was thinking about Ellis Martin and she was thinking about the Chief Inspector who looked rather like Ichabod Crane. And while these people ran through her mind she could not help feeling a merciless little chill when she remembered the pattern of the trees and the stillness broken only by the rustling of leaves that had blown through Tinker Wood.

Chapter
5
.

In the twenty-four hours after she had found Ellis Martin's body, Mary Jepp had been the recipient of more attention from more people than at any other time in her life, and she was not at all sure she liked it. Now, however, it was Sunday morning and life was returning to normal again. It had rained during the night and the garden, still wild and overgrown from the winter, had taken on a distinctly springish quality.

It's true what they say, thought Mary as she let Dog in through the kitchen door, you can smell it coming. Primroses were appearing on the banks by the sides of the lanes. Soon the daffodils would be up and then it would be time for the girl's half-term, a notable landmark in their first year of boarding school. She and Sam had even talked about taking them on a trip at Easter, a surprise holiday. Sam had suggested Florence where they had spent their honeymoon. In Florence at Easter a dove flew through the Duomo and out into the square and a cart full of fireworks was exploded to bring fertility for the coming year. It was just the sort of thing the twins would love, even if they were too young to appreciate the Uffizi. However, if they were going to do all that, they had better decide and book it or else it would be too late. I'll corner Sam today, Mary thought, not that he'll be unwilling. Anything to avoid another stultifying, overstuffed weekend with Mary's mother and her brother's whining wife and numerous children.

Mary was standing at the sink and musing upon just what, exactly, it was that made her sister-in-law so unattractive, when she looked up and saw through the window that a car had turned into the drive. Her first thought was that it was another journalist but they usually drove rather grotty Ford Cotinas and the car driving into the Jepps' courtyard was a large black BMW. Oh hell, Mary thought, it's someone canvassing for the damned by-election, one of Laura Ramsay's minions come to demand that I give a Conservative Club drinks party or help deface the countryside with more wretched placards. She was about to open the window and shout that they voted Alliance when she realized that the man now emerging from the car was not a Conservative Party flunky but Chief Inspector Ross.

It had taken Mary a moment to recognize him because he was wearing corduroys and a fisherman's sweater instead of a dark suit. He now stood in her front yard with his hands in his pockets, looking at her garden. He didn't seem to be making any move toward the house so Mary thought she'd better go out and ask him in. She was just about to go to the door when Sam came around the edge of the house. The two men shook hands and looked solemnly at the newly-turned beds. They frowned as they regarded the tiny daffodil and hyacinth shoots. Mary was just about to go out and ask them what was wrong with her flowers when Sam turned and led the way to the kitchen door.

Ross had come to see the Jepps for a vague set of reasons. This was a tidy murder, right down to the initialed murder weapon. But the motives, the anger and frustration and pain that usually led people to murder, were never tidy. There was nothing neat or orderly about the emotional turbulence that led people to kill. Normally there were physical traces of this turbulence all along the way: bloodstains, broken windows, tipped up furniture, bruises, assault, ripped clothing. But in this case everything was hidden. Owen would check the fiancé's story. He would get a lot of information from him and he would confirm his alibi. And, unless Ross was very much mistaken, that alibi would hold. Without any good reason, purely on instinct, Ross felt that the answers to the questions surrounding Ellis Martin's death lay in this pretty little Kent village where a number of rather prosperous, solid, pleasant people lived in well-kept houses in apparent harmony.

Lying awake last night Ross's mind had circled around and around Ellis Martin and it hadn't taken him long to realize how little he knew about her. He had no real feeling for this pretty blond woman and it was partly for that reason that he had come to see the Jepps. There were reasons that made them a natural choice. They knew most of the people in the village and they felt comfortable with Ross. They were calm and reliable and Ross knew that neither of them had killed Ellis Martin. Their whereabouts on Friday, February fourth, put them out of the running. And Mary Jepp was a sensible, observant woman; she had noticed that Ellis Martin's fingernails had been painted with clear varnish. And besides all that, Ross liked them.

Now they stood beside the Aga in the rather disorderly kitchen while Mary made a pot of coffee.

"What can we do for you, Inspector?" Sam asked as he offered Ross a biscuit.

"I'm not sure," said Ross. They both looked at him, waiting for him to go on. "You see," he continued, "there are things I need to know, but I'm not yet certain as to exactly what they are."

"Ah," said Mary Jepp. She poured the coffee and handed them each a cup.

"I want to know about Ellis Martin," Ross said. He took a sip of the coffee, which was strong. "What kind of person she was, who she knew, who she would have seen—"

Mary Jepp smiled and leaned against the counter. "Who might have a reason for wanting her dead?" she added.

Ross laughed. "Pity the police," he said.

"What kind of person was Ellis?" Mary asked her husband.

Sam Jepp looked at his half-eaten biscuit for a moment and then leaned over and gave it to Dog, who had also been observing it with some interest.

"I don't know," he said. "To be honest that's a rather difficult question."

"You see," said Mary, hoisting herself up onto the counter and sitting there. "Do have a seat, by the way," she added, waving to a kitchen chair. "Ellis really wasn't one of us. I mean, she did live here. She'd lived here as a child. And she did come to drinks parties and shop in the village shop and, well, you know. But she didn't fit in. I can't quite explain it. Except that you'd never have met Ellis popping into the village pub for a half, or chatting about, well, I don't know, whatever it is that people chat about on village streets. It wasn't because she was young and female and single. I mean, Kate's the same age, Kate Davidson up at The Hall. But she's entirely different. There was, well, something cold about Ellis. Maybe because she was blond," Mary added reflectively, helping herself to another biscuit.

"London," said Sam, handing the biscuit packet to Ross.

"I beg your pardon?" Ross said.

"London," Sam said. "That's what I used to think of when I saw Ellis around here. She was, well, city. Rather posh, as they say. Oh, in very good taste, but flashy. The sort of girl you would expect to see working in Sotheby's or Christie's for a bit before she marries a Porsche-driving banker and they move into a flat in the Boltons."

Ross smiled. "Yes," he said, "I see what you mean."

"Ellis always looked right," said Mary. "I mean, she wore barbours and jeans and things, but you knew that her headscarf was Hermes or Gucci or something and she was probably wearing real lingerie underneath it all. She looked like an advertisement for outdoor wear in Country Life, or better yet, The Tatler. Ellis

Martin never had mud on her. That's why I was so certain that she and David would have been a terrible disaster."

Ross looked at Sam Jepp just in time to catch the glance that he threw his wife. She saw it too and waved her hand.

"They'll find out if they don't already know, Sam," she said. She turned to Ross. "David was engaged to Ellis, David Grainger—"

"He's a very good friend of ours," Sam said, breaking in. Ground rules were being laid and Ross was not yet certain as to whether they were for his benefit or for Mary's. Possibly both, he decided.

"Yes," Mary said. "Of course our land borders each other's. David's been a dear friend of ours for years, since we came here. I was, quite frankly, horrified when he got engaged to Ellis. But he was in love with her, or so he said."

"He was," said Sam.

"Not that that does much good. Usually quite the reverse," continued Mary. "Unless you've got the other things that go with it, of course. Like friendship."

"Which they didn't," asked Ross.

"They didn't," said Mary.

"Inspector," said Sam Jepp, "my wife has very firm ideas about things, including what makes up a good marriage."

"Yes, I do," said Mary, "and that would have been a disaster. Of course, she claimed that she loved him, even seemed quite genuine about it all—"

"But you weren't convinced?" asked Ross.

"Not really," said Mary. "I rather think that she

59

just wanted him for some reason. Of course, they had grown up together here and there was the fact that Ellis had no parents and all that. David must have represented all sorts of stability to her, I suppose. But how can you really love someone, in the sense of wanting to marry them, when you seem to want and expect completely different things out of life?" She shook her head and got down off the counter to pour herself another cup of coffee. "Of course," she continued, "he was devastated at the time, when it all came apart. Absolutely devastated."

"What happened?" asked Ross.

"Oh," Mary reached out for his cup which he gave her, "she went off with someone else. Although, do you know—" she stopped and looked out of the window for a moment and then handed Ross his refilled cup and went on, "I always thought that there was more to it than that."

"What do you mean?"

Mary looked at Ross for a moment and then smiled. "I honestly don't know," she said. "That's just what I've always felt."

"Mary has some kind of instinctive radar or sonar, like a bat," said Sam, handing her his cup. "Actually, it's uncanny how often she's proved right."

"I'm sure she is," said Ross.

"In any case," Mary went on, "it was a big mess and everyone was terribly upset. Except, of course, Ellis, who did have the decency to lie low for a bit. It was dreadful. Poor old David. He should have stuck to Kate in the first place."

"Kate?"

Sam nodded. "That's right," he said. "Kate

Davidson. She's a painter, lives up at The Hall. She and David were childhood sweethearts."

"A good deal more than that," said Mary. "That was why everyone was so amazed when he announced that he was going to marry Ellis. Of course, Kate was away in the States at the time, but even so."

"How long ago was all this?" asked Ross, setting his cup down. No wonder Kate didn't like Ellis much, he thought. It's one of the oldest stories in the book.

"Oh, when, Sam?" Mary was asking her husband.

"David and Ellis split up about a year ago," Sam said.

"Before that I suppose that they were engaged for six months or so. And then, of course, it must have been going on for some time before."

"Let me just get this straight," he said. "Ellis Martin and Kate Davidson and David Grainger all grew up here together. At least, in the summers and the holidays?"

Mary nodded. "That was a long time before we came," she said.

"Kate and David were sweethearts, then Kate went to America and while she was away David became engaged to Ellis?"

"That's about right," said Sam. "I daresay it's not uncommon."

"No," said Ross. "But tell me, what was Kate Davidson's reaction to all this?"

"Kate?" asked Mary. "Kate pretends to be frightfully hard and tough as nails. Don't believe it for a moment. She loved David Grainger very much. I think she still does. If he would open his stupid male eyes and get rid of his pride and stop hiding down there on the farm, he'd see it for himself. Stupid man," she added with some feeling. "Kate was heart-broken."

"But not so you'd notice," said Sam. "She's not the type to take her grievances public."

"In fact," said Mary, "if you really want to know much of anything about Ellis from anyone down here, Kate's the person to talk to. Not that there was much love lost between them after all this. But I should think that, apart from David, of course, Kate was the only person down here who really knew her."

"I see," said Ross. "Well, you've been terribly helpful." He stood up and Sam and Mary put down their cups. "I'm sorry to have taken up so much of your time," said Ross, shaking hands. "Thank you for the coffee."

"Not at all," said Mary, following him to the door. "Please come again if there's anything at all that we can do to help. Or even if there isn't," she added, smiling. "We have gin after six."

"Thank you," said Ross.

Halfway to the car Ross stopped and turned back. The Jepps were still standing in the kitchen doorway.

"Can I take it," Ross asked, "that Ellis Martin was not the sort of girl who might have, let's say, had the habit of going out for walks in the countryside?"

Sam shook his head.

"I really wouldn't have thought so," said Mary.

Ross drove through the village, past the green and the sweetshop and the butcher's. The pavements glistened from last night's rain. The publican was opening the front door of The Royal Oak. Ross glanced at his watch. It was just noon. The eleven o'clock family service would be ending any moment now and a large portion of the congregation would probably head for the pub for a mild celebration of another week's worth of virtue.

Ross hated Sundays. The special rituals of family church and lunch and gardening that were so dear to the English heart made him feel more solitary and out of place than any other consequence of his wife's death. Inevitably he woke early on Sunday mornings. Days on duty that hardly mattered. It was on his days off, his precious days of rest, that it became real hell. The twelve hours of confrontation with his own unwelcome solitude would loom ahead of him over the Sunday papers. In the first raw months of her absence, invitations to Sunday lunch could fill him with the shameful background quivering of tears and the ringing of churchbells could only remind him of his own wedding or her death. Now the rawness was gone though the secret dread remained. It did not help, of course, that Kendal had died on a Sunday, that it was on a Sunday morning, to the insistent ringing of the bells of a local church, that Ross had walked for the last time out of the hospital doors into the London street and entered the gray, dead world of grief.

Now Ross used Sundays for his own special footwork, for the private investigations that would not have borne the heavy weight of Owen's presence and ensuing critique. If Ross was going to be wrong about something, he'd just as soon do it on his own time and unobserved. To this end, he hoped and suspected that Kate Davidson would be at home. She didn't seem like the family service type and he couldn't think where else she would be. Unless, of course, she was reading the Sunday papers in bed with David Grainger at Wildesham Place. The thought entered his head without warning and he was annoyed by its presence. Did he really picture them sitting up in a large double bed cradling the deadly weapon between them and discussing their next victim with murderous glee? He couldn't seriously think of her as the Lucrezia Borgia of Wildesham.

Ross hadn't driven to The Hall from the direction of Wildesham before. Yesterday they had approached the house coming from Millbrook. He slowed down to be certain that he didn't miss the entrance to the drive. The road ran downhill and around a corner and then back uphill again. As he started up the hill he saw that the road was covered in mud and clay. Builders' signs and bollards were cluttered along the once pretty banks of the lane. Someone was cutting a wide entrance road, far bigger than a driveway, into the hillside. It made a large, ugly hole where trees had been ripped out and the earth had been flattened to make way for yet more of the concrete that seemed to be covering the entire country. The thought of it made Ross both irritable and depressed and, as a result, he nearly drove past a narrow, graveled drive that was flanked by two tall Italianate pillars. He braked. It wasn't the front drive of the house, which he was certain was wider and lined by trees. This must be the back drive. He turned in and drove slowly up the hill.

The drive wound through pasture and approached the back of the house in a gentle arc. When The Hall was built this would have been parkland. Now it was mowed and planted in daffodils. In a month or so there would be a wash of yellow leading up to the mellowing brick. It must be very beautiful, he thought, just the kind of thing that Kendal would have loved.

The drive ended in a small courtyard and there, sure enough, were several garages. It wasn't until Ross had got out of the car and started to walk away that the flash of color caught his eye. One of the garage doors was ajar. When he pulled it back he saw an old, beetle-shaped Porsche 911. Bright red. There wouldn't be two of those in Wildesham. Grainger must have rung her immediately, Ross thought, as soon as he got back into the house, directly after Mary Jepp had told him that the body in the wood was Ellis Martin.

Ross pushed the door closed and followed the path around the garage. Here and there flower beds were laid out and kept as meticulously as the herb garden. Beyond, there was a small pond and, to the side of that, a new building that could only be a studio. Ross started out across the lawn, his shoes leaving dark footprints on the turf.

She must have seen him, possibly been expecting him, because she opened the door before he was halfway there and watched him come toward her. Today she had traded the black for a pink cotton jumper and a pair of distinctly grubby trousers with paint on them. She had also left her hair down and standing there in the doorway of her studio she looked either like a pre-Raphaelite angel in chinos or Lady Macbeth out to do a bit of gardening.

"Good morning, Chief Inspector," she said, smiling. "Do come in."

The studio was dominated by a large triptych whose panels reached almost from ceiling to floor. Each panel was covered with what, on first glance, appeared to be a frieze of flowers. The center was lilies, the left irises, the right daffodils. The colors, predominantly reds, yellows, and oranges, were bitten with the green of the leaves and ran riot, as if the entire piece was in the process of being consumed by flames. On closer inspection, Ross saw that there were faces amid the flowers: cats' faces. Leopards for the irises, tigers amid the lillies, and lions in the daffodils. Their eyes stared out at him, brown and soft and haunted from their jungle of blossom.

Kate disappeared behind the panel. She stuck her head around the right-hand side and said, "Sorry, I've been stretching canvases. It's almost as good as weightlifting." She glanced at the lion panel and smiled. "See the resemblance?" Before Ross could comment she emerged and stood beside him looking at the triptych. "I don't quite know what to call it," she said. "Cat bouquet? Feline Flora? Anyway, I suspect that you didn't come here to view my work."

"I'm sorry, no," Ross said.

"I'm done in here for now." She opened the door and motioned for him to go ahead. "Let's go up to the house." Ross stepped outside and she followed him, locking the door behind her. In the daylight he noticed that she looked tired. There were smudges under her eyes that could have been charcoal, but weren't.

"Well, Chief Inspector," she said as they started across the lawn, "what can I do for you?"

Ross looked at her. "I want you to tell me about Ellis Martin."

After refusing yet more coffee, Ross followed Kate into the library at the back of the house. The walls were lined with bookshelves and there was a television and a built-in bar. French windows looked out over the lawn.

"This is my evening room," said Kate, sitting down in one of the armchairs. She had taken a packet of cigarettes from the bar and now she peeled the cellophane off carefully and tapped the bottom of the box. Ross sat on the sofa and waited. Kate lit the cigarette and deposited the match neatly in the ashtray on the coffee table before she looked at Ross.

"I'm assuming," she said, "that someone's told you the story?"

Ross nodded. "If you mean about David Grainger, yes. At least partially. I'd rather hear it from you."

"I see." She looked out of the window, blowing smoke in little puffs. In the afternoon light, with her hair down, Ross thought she looked older than he had remembered. Already there were thin papery lines along the corners of her eyes. Her profile was just short of beautiful. The nose was a little too long, the mouth slightly too wide.

"It's an old story," she said, looking back at him.

"They usually are," said Ross.

She was clearly trying to make up her mind. About what she would tell him? How she would tell him? She unfolded herself from the chair and went to the bar.

"I don't know about you," she said, "but in my book it's past noon on a Sunday and the combination of that and talking about Ellis calls for a drink."

"All right," Ross agreed. "I'm not on duty. A very weak gin and tonic would be lovely."

She made the drinks and smiled as she handed him the glass.

"Thank you," she said, sitting down. "Makes it seem less like an inquisition."

"Miss Davidson," Ross said quickly, "you're under no obligation to talk to me. You do realize that? I'm not here in an official capacity. If you would prefer it, I'll leave."

"And return tomorrow in an official capacity with your little Welsh alter ego in tow? No, Chief Inspector. All of this is going to come out in any case. It's just as well that it be now. It's such a public business, isn't it—having someone murdered? That is what it is, isn't it?" she added. "I mean, no one's actually said, but we are all assuming that Ellis didn't dig a hole and shoot herself so as to fall into it?"

"No," Ross said, "I think we can count that out."

"Yes," said Kate. "Well, just as well to be sure." She had settled back into the armchair. Taking a sip of her drink, she said, "I'm not sure, really, that there's all that much to tell. I used to go out with David Grainger. I went off to the States to complete my MFA. He fell in love with Ellis and they got engaged. End of story."

"I see." Ross rolled his glass between his hands, watching the ice melt into the gently fizzing tonic. "Why?" he asked.

"Why what?" She was watching him from behind a veil of cigarette smoke. Like the lions, he thought. She was right, there was a resemblance.

"Why did Ellis change her mind?"

Kate laughed. "Why did Ellis ever do anything? Why is the sky blue and the moon made of green cheese? I'm damned if I know, Inspector. As I told you, at that point in time Ellis wasn't exactly taking me into her confidence."

"And David Grainger?"

"We weren't particularly close just then either, as you can imagine."

"And now?"

"Now?" She stubbed the cigarette out carefully. "Now David and I are friends. Time passes, things change. People forget."

Ross wasn't quite so sure. This woman didn't strike him as the forgetful type.

"And David never talked to you about it afterward? Never told you why it was that Ellis broke off the engagement?"

"Inspector," Kate said, "there are some things that you have to understand about Ellis for any of this to make sense. The first is that she was actually not a very nice person. Oh, she was lovely at times, when it suited her. Ellis was quite convinced, you see, that the world revolved around her, that it was, in fact, centrally balanced on a point called Ellis Martin. And if Ellis chose to include you in her world, then you had the distinct feeling that the world also revolved around you. That can be quite satisfying, if you like that sort of thing. But God help you if you got in Ellis's way, if you see what I mean. Ellis didn't really care for other people. Let's just say that the word 'compassion' was not writ large in her vocabulary."

"Was she intelligent?" asked Ross.

Kate looked at him with something like surprise, as if he were a child who had suddenly and uncharacteristically asked a perceptive question.

"That's an interesting question," she said. "In a way, yes. Almost in the way that terribly self-centered people have to be intelligent." Kate paused and thought for a moment. "She wasn't intelligent in the sense of intellect. You wouldn't have caught Ellis reading Plato of an afternoon, or thinking about the moral nature of art. But she did have an extraordinary amount of what my mother always calls 'native cunning.' Ellis always made certain that Ellis came out on top. Although," Kate added, reaching for another cigarette, "it does rather look as though somewhere along the way she might have made a mistake."

Ross put his glass down on the table carefully. Unless he was much mistaken, there was something very close to satisfaction lingering around Kate's last remark. She was watching him again. Waiting, perhaps, for him to ask if she was glad that Ellis Martin was dead. He didn't feel that the question was necessary. Instead, he said, "What else was there about her? I mean as a person—"

Kate nodded. "She was manipulative," she said. "You have to be to be that successful at getting what you want. Ellis knew instinctively what people's weak points were and she saved them up. She never forgot, in case the knowledge came in handy at a later date."

"What else?"

"A troublemaker." Kate smiled. "Actually, that was one of her more endearing qualities, one of the things that made her at least a little bit human. Ellis liked a little trouble. It livened things up. I think she found it pretty dull down here most of the time. It's not exactly socially thrilling. I think that Ellis took pleasure, from time to time, in giving the pot a little stir. She was good at it too. Sometimes it was quite a pleasure to watch."

"I see," said Ross. "And what did you do? After Ellis and David got engaged?"

She shrugged. "I did what all pathetic, abandoned women do. I carried on with my life."

Ross stood up. "Thank you, Miss Davidson," he said. "You've been most helpful. I'm sorry to intrude on your Sunday."

"That's all right, it's a pleasure." She got up and opened the French windows for him. "I'll walk you to your car," she said.

As they stepped out onto the bricked terrace, Ross paused and looked across the garden. On the far side of the back drive, across the field, there was a line of tall, silvery trees. They reminded him of the tourist brochure pictures of French country roads. Beyond them a hedge was being put in to mask the raw, ugly gash of the building site that was being dug out on the other side.

"It's vile, isn't it?" Kate said. "This is a designated rural area and those stupid bastards on the planning board simply don't give a damn. We were hoping that the by-election would make a difference, but I don't think there's much of a chance that it will, realistically speaking."

"Oh, yes," said Ross, "Aury Blaire, wasn't it?" If Ross remembered correctly, Blaire had dropped dead quite suddenly of a heart attack right in the middle of his term in parliament. The by-election to find a new MP for the area to take Blaire's place had only been announced recently. Already Ross had noticed placards promoting one candidate or another going up in the surrounding villages. Voting was due to take place in about six weeks' time.

"That's right," Kate was saying, "Blaire had been the local MP for centuries. An old-fashioned Conservative, you know, the gentlemanly type, a bit dotty but liked the birds and wildflowers. He'd already gotten railroaded by the new 'money at any cost' crowd over the planning permission for this monstrosity. Still, when he dropped dead last month and they had to call the by-election, we did hope that there might be some chance of the Alliance getting in."

"No hope?" he asked.

She shook her head. "Not really. This is a safe Conservative seat and with Laura Ramsay running, or rather steamrolling, for it, it's pretty much sewed up. Laura's our local Conservative Iron Lady. A real Matron from Hell, she seems to feel it's her personal responsibility to carry on Maggie's legacy no matter what the cost. She adores this depot, anything for progress. Funnily enough," she added, "that was about the one thing that Ellis and I did see eye to eye on."

"What's it going to be?" asked Ross, nodding toward the building site.

"A depot for a haulage company, if you can believe it," Kate said. "We did everything we could to try to stop it. But, as we all know, planning has virtually nothing to do with democracy and everything to do with making a buck. You-know-who's legacy to Britain." She turned and began walking toward the garages. Ross followed her.

"Miss Davidson," he said, "does the name Clara Beale mean anything to you?"

"No," Kate said. "Should it?"

"I shouldn't think so," said Ross.

At the car she shook his hand and smiled.

"Come again," she said, "if there's anything at all that I can do."

"There is one more thing." Ross paused with his hand on the door handle. "I don't suppose that you remember where you were on the afternoon of Friday, February fourth? From about noon onward?"

"As a matter of fact, I do," Kate said. "I went for a walk." The smile spread slowly across her face, creasing the fine lines around her eyes and revealing what might once have been a dimple. "It was a particularly lovely day. I wanted the exercise. I walked from here to a pub called The Snipe, in May Green. I left at about noon and I don't think that I was back until around about half past three."

"The Snipe?" Ross asked.

"That's right," said Kate. "It's just on the other side of Tinker Wood."

Chapter 6.

By The Holy God, this is a bloody awful job," said Owen, taking his coat off and hanging it over the back of one of the quasi-oak chairs in Ross's office. "Miranda keeps telling me that I do it because I love it and I just tell her she's mad. I suppose you do it because you love it, do you?"

Ross put his pen down and pushed his chair back from the desk. He silently regarded Owen.

"Well you're mad too," said Owen and he threw himself down on top of his coat and closed his eyes. Ross waited.

"I met him at Gatwick," Owen said. "Poor bastard, he hadn't a clue. I'm afraid I couldn't get much out of him that was useful."

"No," said Ross, "I suppose not, just now."

"He was in Spain—at some film festival or other—the entire time. Left on the first, came back this morning. I'm having it all checked."

74

"It'll wash," said Ross.

Owen opened his eyes and looked at him. "What makes you so bloody sure?" he asked.

Ross smiled and tapped his forehead.

"Oh God," Owen groaned. "Not another bout of the famous instinct?"

"I'm afraid so," said Ross.

Owen got up and went to the door. Poking his head around it, he shouted for coffee. Then he came back and slumped in the chair again, but this time he was smiling.

"So, Master," he said, "what's it been telling you?"

"Before all that," said Ross, "tell me about the fiancé."

"William Thomas DeWarre," said Owen. "Aged 32. Nice chap, as a matter of fact. Works for the British Film Institute, something to do with admin. Not really an arty type." Ross assumed this to mean that he didn't wear earrings or an off-white linen suit.

"He met Ellis over a year ago," Owen continued, "at some dinner party or other in London. They'd been engaged a few months, the date was set for June. He last saw her the day he left, February first. She drove him to the airport. He knew about the film course in Canterbury, put her on to it. Thought she might enjoy it. He'd not tried to ring her there during the week. He was expecting her to pick him up at the airport this morning. Apparently he had no idea that anything was amiss."

"I see," said Ross.

"I'm sorry," said Owen. "I didn't have the heart to push further. Not just then. The poor bastard had had about as much as he could take. I had the police take him home. He lives in Hampstead and he's coming down here early tomorrow morning. He wanted to talk to you so I told him you'd be in first thing."

There was a knock on the door and Constable Barry Glen came in carrying a tray with a pot of coffee and two cups on it. Now that the Martin house had been gone over and closed up, Barry was back on station duty. He'd volunteered to work overtime because it wasn't so often that you got a chance to be around people like Chief Inspector Ross and, as Angie always said, you had to make the most of the opportunities that God gave you in this life. To that end Constable Glen was pleased that he managed to set the tray down without spilling anything. Angie had trained him well.

After Ross had poured the coffee and handed a cup to Owen, he gave a brief description of his morning's visits.

When he was finished, Owen placed his cup carefully back on the tray. "Well, well, well," he said. "And does that bring you to motive?"

Ross thought for a moment. "I'm not altogether certain," he said, "on Kate Davidson's part."

"Walking through Tinker Wood and all, was she? She's a cool customer, that lady."

"Yes," said Ross, "she's a very interesting woman. But at this moment I think it's time we pay a visit to Mr. Grainger and have a word with him about a certain spade."

David Grainger reminded Ross of Heathcliff. He was tall and dark with curly black hair. There was no doubt that he and Kate Davidson must have made a very striking couple. Heathcliff and Cathy, in the wood, with a spade. Oh, for God's sake, Ross said to himself.

They were standing in the main yard of the farm at Wildesham Place, which bore no resemblance at all to Wuthering Heights. It was utterly immaculate. David Grainger obviously took his farming very seriously indeed. He shook hands with Ross and Owen and said, "I'm glad to meet you. How can I help?"

"I understand, sir," said Ross, "that you were an old friend of Ellis Martin's."

David Grainger smiled. It was a warm, open smile.

"You could say that, Chief Inspector," he said. "You could also say that I was once planning to marry her, as I'm sure you're aware by now."

"Yes," said Ross, "we had heard something of the kind."

David Grainger shrugged. "Villages are small places. That's what I like about them. Yes, Chief Inspector, I was a very old friend of Ellis Martin's."

"When did you see her last?" asked Owen.

"As a matter of fact, I hadn't seen her in almost a year, since the night we split up, if you want to know exactly. That is, not to talk to," he added. "I think I actually saw her last some few weeks ago. Perhaps as much as two months ago now. It was at a meeting to protest over this new haulage depot. The one they're building at the other side of the village."

"Next to the Davidson house," said Ross.

"That's right," said David. "An appalling thing. Ruining the entire village."

"Something you and Ellis Martin agreed on?"

"Yes." David smiled again. "The strangest things

will bring people together, won't they? As a matter of fact, that was something that Ellis felt very strongly about, not that I suppose it matters now."

"Why was it," asked Ross, "that you and Ellis Martin broke off your engagement?"

The question seemed to startle David Grainger. He paused for a moment and then said, "Well, who knows what goes through a woman's head? Ellis changed her mind, Inspector. What more can I say?"

"Quite," said Ross.

"Tell me, sir," said Owen, "do you have your farm equipment, your spades and shovels and such, branded?"

"Yes," said Grainger, "as a matter of fact, I do. I had them all marked just over a year ago. There was a rash of thefts in the area. I think most people had their farm equipment marked."

"And can you tell me, sir," asked Owen, "what the particular marking for this farm is?"

"Of course," said David. "As a matter of fact, I can do better than that. I can show you." He disappeared into a shed and emerged a moment later carrying a pitchfork. "Here," he said, showing them a marking just above the prongs, "you can see. They're all marked the same way, with a W and a P for the farm's name."

"And could you be missing a spade, sir? Without noticing it perhaps?" asked Owen.

David Grainger's face went quite pale and for a moment Ross was afraid he might faint. He seemed to sway slightly on his feet before he regained his balance.

"Oh, no," he said. "Oh no, not—"

"Yes, I'm afraid so, sir," said Owen. "It was found in the old cottage, or rather, close by it."

"Oh, my poor Ellis," David said. "My poor, silly girl."

They waited for a moment until he spoke again.

"I haven't missed one in particular," he said, "but there are an awful lot of them about. My barns and sheds are almost never locked."

"So," said Ross, "it would be easy for someone to steal one?"

David Grainger nodded.

"That's right," he said. "I've only a few men working here and they're out in the fields most of the time, at least recently. And, of course, this yard is quite a ways from the house. It would be easy to get in and out without being noticed."

"Yes, I see," said Ross. "Thank you, Mr. Grainger, for giving us so much of your time. We may want to speak with you again." Grainger nodded.

"Of course," he said. "Anything I can do."

"Oh, there is one more thing," said Owen. "Could you be so good as to tell us where you were on the afternoon of Friday, February fourth, from noon onward?

Grainger paused for a moment.

"Of course," he said. "I was here, working on the farm."

"Thank you, Mr. Grainger," said Ross. "You've been very helpful."

It was almost midnight when Ross finally turned off the stereo and decided to try to get some sleep. He had been re-reading Dante. It always fascinated him to be reminded of who, exactly, had been placed in which circle of Hell.

As he slipped the *Faure Requiem* gently back into its plastic casing, he thought of Kendal. This had been one of her favorite pieces of music, part of the selection she had chosen for her funeral. It had seemed to take her so long to die, Ross thought. How could he be so cruel as to wish for her back, wish for her to have to go through all of that again? She had always seemed so small to him, like a bird or a doll. Now, sometimes, he was gripped by a sense of panic as he felt her receding down the years, moving further and further away from him, sinking through layers of time until he felt he could barely see her.

The telephone interrupted with a ring that was particularly loud and unpleasant in the silent house. It was Owen.

"You weren't asleep," he asked.

"No," said Ross.

"Good. Look, I don't know what you'll make of this, but I thought I ought to let you know so you could have time to think about it before you see the boyfriend tomorrow. May not be important, who knows?" He paused for a moment and then continued. "The thing is that the autopsy report came in this evening, just before I left. I took the liberty of taking it home with me. I was going to have it for you first thing in the morning. Hope you don't mind?"

"No," said Ross. "Go ahead."

"Well, I've just got through with it," said Owen. "On the whole, entirely unremarkable, except for one thing. Apparently Ellis Martin had been pregnant. Recently too. Say, within the last year."

Chapter

7.

"What?" asked William DeWarre. "Are you absolutely certain? There can't be a mistake?"

"I'm afraid not, Mr. DeWarre," said Ross. "There's no doubt about it. I take it that you were not aware? That the baby wasn't yours?"

William DeWarre shook his head. "No," he said. "No, I wasn't aware. And I'm positive that it wasn't mine. Ellis would have told me. Even if she hadn't, she wouldn't have been able to hide it from me. But that's ridiculous in any case. Ellis would have told me."

"But it could have been before you met her?" Ross asked. "You'd known her how long? A year?"

"We met, well, ten months ago, really. Yes, it must have been, the baby, before I met her."

William DeWarre had been sitting in Ross's office for almost an hour. He had arrived, as promised, by 9:00 A.M. Ross had been surprised that he was such an ordinary looking man, not that he had exactly been expecting anything else. He supposed that somewhere in the back of his head he must have had an image of DeWarre, of someone young and arty and unfortunately given to peppering conversations with references to film noir and the scripts of Claude Chabrol. But DeWarre was none of these things. He was a pleasant, ordinary looking young man in a tweed jacket whose fiancée had just been murdered.

For the last hour he had gone over his own movements in detail with Ross. Ellis had spent the day with him on February first, had driven him to the airport in the evening. He had arrived in Madrid and spent the night, driving south the next morning to the small town where the film festival was held. He had spent the following ten days watching films, going to cocktail parties and voting as a member of the jury. Already Owen was tracing the car rental, tracing his movements, quietly checking on this rather unremarkable story to see if there was any moment, any space of a day or so when he had disappeared, when he could have returned to England to hit Ellis Martin on the head with a spade in Tinker Wood. Both Ross and Owen knew that this was highly unlikely, but they couldn't afford to overlook the possibility.

Having covered the routine account of DeWarre's movements, Ross offered him another cup of coffee and set off on the tack that really interested him. For what seemed like the hundredth time since Saturday morning, he shifted in his distinctly uncomfortable chair and said, "Tell me about Ellis Martin."

DeWarre put his cup down on the edge of the desk and looked out of the window. Ross saw that his hands were shaking slightly in his lap.

"Forgive me," DeWarre said. "All of this seems so completely unreal. Yesterday morning I flew into Gatwick expecting to see Ellis standing there and today I'm sitting here telling you what she used to be like because she's dead. And now I don't even know what I know. I was going to marry the woman in a few months time and I didn't even have any idea that within the last year she must have had either an abortion, a miscarriage, or—" He stopped and looked helplessly at Ross.

"I think we can count that out," Ross said quietly. He wasn't certain whether the expression that chased across DeWarre's face was relief or further anguish.

"It's true, isn't it, Inspector, all those things they say about how you never really know people?"

"Yes," said Ross, "I think it is. Tell me about the Ellis that you knew."

"She was beautiful. That's very male, isn't it? But it was part of her. It was something that you noticed about her immediately, how beautiful she was. She could be very funny. She was intelligent. She was a very powerful person, in her own way. Very determined, if she believed in something, or wanted something. I respected her enormously for that. Ellis wasn't someone who just let life happen to her. She went out and went after it."

"What about her friends?" asked Ross.

DeWarre shrugged. "She had some friends down here, not that I really knew them. Most of them were older, you know, people her aunt had known in the village, that sort of thing. As a matter of fact we went to a drinks party on New Year's Day with a couple who'd known her aunt. Ramsay or something, I think. It was a bit odd, actually. Not the drinks party, the fact that, now that I think about it, it doesn't seem to me that Ellis had many friends. After we got together she spent most of her time with my friends. I didn't think about it, really."

"I see," said Ross. "Then tell me something else. What did Ellis do? I mean with her time? With her days?"

DeWarre laughed. "Oh Inspector," he said, "I suppose that Ellis did what wealthy girls do. She didn't work because she didn't have to and she didn't want to. She kept my flat in London. She went to art galleries, she went shopping, I suppose she went to lunch. She planned our wedding. She came down here. She adored her house, you know, the one in Wildesham. She spent a lot of time here, working in the garden. Or rather, organizing her gardener to work in the garden. She was interested in landscaping. It was one of the things I tried to encourage her to do more of. I thought that perhaps, after we were married, she might want to take some serious courses, maybe do a degree."

"And the film?" asked Ross.

"Yes," said DeWarre. "Yes, she got very interested in that, particularly in documentary. In fact, we'd recently gone a bit mad on it, hence the Canterbury course. Of course, I screen films all the time and Ellis came to a lot of them with me. We were doing a special series on classic documentaries at the BFI, or rather, getting ready to do one. We were screening everything that we own to see what to include. Ellis loved that. In fact, she used to come in and screen things on her own sometimes. You know, in viewing booths."

"I see," said Ross. None of this, he thought, was being particularly helpful. It seemed to be the things that William DeWarre didn't know about Ellis Martin that were more revealing than what he did know. Still, the questions had to be asked.

"I'm afraid I have to ask you," said Ross. "Why would someone want to murder Ellis Martin?"

DeWarre shook his head. "I have absolutely no idea," he said.

Ross walked DeWarre out to his car.

"I'll be staying down here," DeWarre said, "for the inquest tomorrow and perhaps for a day or two after. I've booked a room at the Cavendish House, the country house hotel place, if you need me for anything."

"Thank you," said Ross. "Tell me, Mr. DeWarre, do you know someone called Clara Beale?"

"Clara Beale?" DeWarre stood by the car, fingering his keys and thought for a moment. "Do you know," he said, "the name is terribly familiar? But I can't think why."

"An acquaintance? Friend of a friend? Employee at the film institute?"

DeWarre shook his head. "No," he said, "I don't think so."

"Perhaps someone Ellis mentioned? Or who did some work for her, altered a dress, arranged flowers, cut her hair?"

"I don't know," said DeWarre. "But it does seem familiar. Is it important?"

"I'm not sure," said Ross. "I shouldn't think so. It's just a loose end that I'd like to clear up. If you do remember?"

"Of course," said DeWarre, "I'll let you know at once. There is one more thing—" He stopped fiddling with his keys and looked down at his hands. After a moment he looked at Ross again and said, "Is it all right for me to go to the house? I don't mean to stay there. I have no idea who owns it now. I just wanted to—" He bit his lip and looked away across the parking lot.

"I don't see that that's a problem," said Ross. "We're finished there."

"Thank you," said DeWarre. "You've been very kind."

"I'll see you at the inquest tomorrow," said Ross, shaking his hand. "And if there's anything that I can do for you, you can reach me here."

DeWarre began to get into his car.

"Oh, Mr. DeWarre," Ross called. "I'm sorry, but there is just one last thing. Could you tell me if the names David Grainger and Kate Davidson mean anything to you?"

DeWarre thought for a moment and then shook his head. "No," he said, "I'm afraid they don't mean a thing."

Ross stood for a moment and watched William DeWarre's blue Peugeot weave its way down the crowded main street, then he turned on his heel and went back into the station.

Owen was on the telephone when Ross appeared beside him. Ross was already wearing his overcoat and he was holding Owen's. Owen cut the call short and followed Ross out the door.

"Where are we going?" Owen asked as he got into Ross's passenger seat.

"To see David Grainger." Ross was already turning into the main street. "DeWarre says the baby wasn't his," said Ross without looking at Owen, "and I believe he's right."

The day was bright and balmy, more like April than February, but as they drove through the lanes toward Wildesham Place, Ross wasn't thinking about the weather. He had realized quite suddenly that he was intensely annoyed and that the person he was annoyed with was Kate Davidson. He was absolutely certain that she knew about Ellis Martin's baby. Ellis Martin's baby must also have been David Grainger's baby. And yet she hadn't told him. She had, in fact, lied to him when she had said that she had no idea why Ellis ended the engagement. You have no evidence for any of that, Ross told himself. No, he replied, but I know it's true. Why did he expect her to tell the truth in any case? Why, on earth, was he so offended that she had lied to him? Didn't everyone lie to the police? Ross suspected that David Grainger hadn't told him the truth either and that didn't seem to bother him. He couldn't decide whether, in fact, he was more angry with Kate for lying to him or with himself for being annoyed about it. He didn't have much time to dwell on the question, since they were presently turning into the driveway of Wildesham Place.

David Grainger was in the farm office, going through the books, when Owen and Ross arrived. He came out to meet them.

"Good morning, Inspector," he called. "What can I do to help you?"

Ross got out of the car and paused for a moment.

"I wonder," he said, "if you might be able to tell me about Ellis Martin's baby?"

David Grainger looked at Ross and his face suddenly seemed to grow older. It was a look that Ross knew well and one that he had not expected. He felt a flinch of guilt that he had not been kinder. David Grainger's face was caved in with sorrow.

"The autopsy?" he asked.

"Yes," said Ross.

David looked away, nodding. "I suppose I knew they'd be able to tell. What do you want me to say, Inspector?" He turned back to Ross. "It was just about a year ago that Ellis got pregnant. I wanted her to have the baby. She didn't want it. About then she decided that she didn't want me either. She got rid of it. The whole thing came to an end. I begged her not to. I pleaded with her, but she wasn't having a bit of it. She said she didn't want the responsibility."

"And that was when she broke off the engagement?"

"That's right. We could hardly walk down the aisle after that, could we?"

"I'm terribly sorry," said Ross.

David Grainger shook his head and smiled. "So am I, Inspector. So am I."

In the car, Owen turned to Ross. "I think that perhaps we'd better get to talking with people who might have seen David Grainger after, say, noon on the fourth," he said.

"Yes," Ross agreed, "I think we'd better."

They were driving through Wildesham. Some bicycles and a few cars were parked outside of the village shops. In the sunshine, the whole thing looked like something off a postcard. Ross couldn't help thinking that the Channel Tunnel was going to make mincemeat of this whole part of the country. Perhaps the desecration wouldn't actually reach this far, but surely the haulage depot was indication enough of what was on the way.

As they approached the crossroads on the far side of the village, Ross suddenly braked. There was a small commotion going on by the side of the road and an ambulance from the local cottage hospital was pulling up. Owen got out of the car and, reaching for his identification wallet, stepped through the knot of onlookers. Ross followed.

A child of perhaps twelve or thirteen lay on the verge of the road, her face white with pain. An older woman knelt beside her, talking to her quietly and moving her hands gently down the girl's left leg. A bicycle lay a few feet away, half under the hedgerow. Behind him, Ross could hear Owen talking to a local constable. The girl, it seemed, had cycled onto the crossing without looking, swerved to avoid a car and skidded across the road. While Ross watched, the woman carefully unlaced the girl's shoe and removed it.

The St. John's ambulance crew, a middle-aged man followed by a rather timid-looking boy, came trotting up.

"Well, well, well," said the man heartily, "and what have we here?"

"What you have here," said the woman without taking her eyes off of the child, "is a fracture of the left tibia and some rather nasty abrasions to go with it. It has already begun to swell." She looked up at him with a gaze that challenged him to disagree. Ross noticed that she was wearing a dress and no coat. Her shoes were polished. He wondered if she were cold.

"I see," said the ambulance man, "and you're a doctor, are you, Madame?" The child made a pained mewing sound. The woman glanced at her and turned back to the ambulance crew.

"No," she said, "I am not a doctor and neither are you. You are a St. John's ambulance medic and if you don't get a move on and put an air splint on this child's leg, you are going to have rather a mess on your hands."

The medic began to reply, thought better of it, and instead knelt down to feel the girl's leg for himself.

Owen materialized beside Ross.

"All under control," he said. "No one else involved. He's got the driver's statement, local chap. Shall we?" Owen turned away toward Ross's car. As Ross turned to follow him, he saw the woman appropriate the medical shears and snip through the left seam of the girl's jeans with swift, deft strokes.

Ross started the car and they continued out of Wildesham toward The Hall. The depot site was coming up on their right. An earth digger came out of the access drive to the site. It lumbered onto the road just as Ross came around the corner and he had to swerve rather more quickly than he would have liked in order to avoid careening into it.

"Jesus!" said Owen. "That's bloody lethal, that is! Why in hell do they let them build things like that? Someone's going to get killed."

"Yes," said Ross, "I should think they are."

"Planning committees ought to be shot," said Owen, summing up the problem succinctly as they turned into the back drive of The Hall.

Ross drove up the gentle sweep of the drive and parked the car behind the garages. He turned to Owen.

"Wait for me here, would you?" he asked. "I'll only be a minute." He got out of the car and walked quickly across the lawn toward the studio.

She was there, all right, working on the last panel of the triptych. She turned and smiled at him as he opened the door and said, "Why the hell didn't you tell me about Ellis Martin's baby?"

She was holding her pallet in one hand and a brush in the other. She stood in the sunlight, posed like a Victorian allegory of "Woman As Art."

"Because I didn't think that it was any of your goddamn business," she said.

They stood glaring at each other until Kate put the pallet and brush down and said, "How nice to see you, Chief Inspector. Won't you come in?"

Ross came into the studio, closing the door behind him. He no longer felt angry, just slightly deflated and rather silly.

"I'm sorry," he said. "I do apologize, Miss Davidson, but surely you realize that everything about Ellis Martin is our business."

"Yes," Kate said, "I'm beginning to see that. I didn't tell you because of David."

"I understand," said Ross. "Do you think that you can tell me now?"

"Yes," she said, "if you like." She sat down on a stool and looked at him. "Ellis got pregnant," she said. "They were going to be married in a few months anyway and David was delighted. He was completely thrilled and he desperately wanted the baby. David's rather a solitary person, you see, Inspector, and you have to be so frightfully careful with people like that, don't you? Everyone thinks that they're terribly tough, but if you get to them, they're the easiest of all to hurt. As a matter of fact, it's probably unavoidable, one way or another. In any case, Ellis really got to him. I never did. Not like that." She paused and brushed a strand of hair out of her eyes. There was paint on the back of her hands. She went on. "Ellis didn't give a damn," she said. "She just didn't want the baby and that was that. It might have intruded on her perfect picture of her perfect life. God knows what she thought marriage was going to be like. In any case, she decided that she wasn't going to have the baby and that, on second thoughts, she didn't want David either. He literally begged her to have it, said he'd keep it himself, the whole lot. Some rather horrible things were said, or so I gather. That's what he couldn't ever understand, why she felt the need to be so cruel about it. You see, he thought of her, well, she was the woman he was going to marry. She just turned off cold. She made it very plain that she had no interest whatsoever in him or his baby." Kate got up from her stool and lit a cigarette.

"It's a sordid little story," she said, blowing out the match. "I thought he was going to kill himself. He called me because he didn't really have anyone else to call. I stayed with him that night and for a few nights afterward. I've never seen anyone in so much pain." She took a long drag off the cigarette and blew two perfect smoke rings. "I hadn't hated Ellis until then," she said. "As a matter of fact, I hadn't ever hated anyone. But that was exactly when I started to hate Ellis Martin. Date. Time. Hour. David will never be the same again. You don't recover from something like that. You just try to go beyond it. And she just didn't give a goddamn."

Kate looked at him and smiled. "Oh yes, Inspector," she said. "I know what you're thinking. And you're right. I could quite happily have killed Ellis Martin."

They stood looking at each other across the cluttered, sunbathed studio.

"And did you?" asked Ross.

"No," she said, "I didn't."

Chapter
8.

Owen balanced on the edge of his chair and stuck his legs out in front of him. He surveyed the toes of his polished shoes thoughtfully, then he said, "We have a woman who was engaged to a childhood friend. A childhood friend, mind you, that she'd nicked from another childhood friend, so to speak. We have a woman who gets pregnant and chucks her fiancé without so much as a by-your-leave, gets rid of the brat-to-be and goes off and gets re-engaged to someone else. No problem there, incidentally. Fiancé Mark II has an airtight alibi and no discernible motive. She's a strange egg, though, our Ellis. Doesn't tell her new fiancé about the old one, about the possible baby or, it would appear, about much of anything at all."

"Not what you'd call open," said Ross.

"Not exactly warm and forthcoming," said Owen. "But, let us continue. Forensics, so far, gives us nothing. Pathology gives us not very much. Nothing

93

apart from the baby business. Oh, and the fact that she had nothing in her stomach. She did not eat lunch on the fourth. Not that that proves much of anything, least of all that she was dead at lunchtime. A lot of women who aren't dead don't eat lunch. So, we conclude that Ellis Martin left her house of her own free will sometime after twelve noon on Friday, February fourth. There are no signs of a struggle in the house, therefore——" Owen waved his hand in the air.

"Agreed," said Ross, "go on."

"She could have driven herself," Owen said, "at a great stretch. But it's highly unlikely. The car is completely clean. The only fingerprints in it are hers or DeWarre's. So, if someone drove it back to the house after killing her, they were careful beyond belief and they managed to do it in a highly visible car in a small village. We can count that out, I think. Either Ellis was taken to Tinker Wood or, if she got there herself, she walked. Let's deal with the first alternative. If she was taken by someone else we can brilliantly deduce that she was either dead or alive. If she was dead our killer would have had to load her into a vehicle of some sort. We can pretty safely assume it's a car, and drive her up there after having bashed her on the head with a spade. Presumably the spade would have been dumped in the wood at the same time——"

"They did use it to dig the grave?" Ross asked. "The spade, I mean."

"Probable," said Owen. "That would be as tidy as everything else."

"Yes," said Ross. "Not much's been wasted here, has it? No extra mess."

"Where do you think she was killed?" asked Owen.

"I'm not altogether certain," said Ross. "I suspect it

was in Tinker Wood. Otherwise the risk involved in moving the body is substantial. It's not an easy thing to do and a gash like that causes a bit of a mess."

"This is all assuming that someone meant to kill her, that she wasn't just bashed over the head with a spade in the heat of argument," said Owen.

"Correct," said Ross. "Working on that assumption, if someone planned to kill her in Tinker Wood they either had to persuade her to go up there with them or persuade her to meet them there. If she went to meet them it would mean that she walked, which is certainly possible, though apparently unlikely."

"Fratelli Rossetti," said Owen.

"I beg your pardon?"

Owen smiled. "Fratelli Rossetti. Very expensive Italian shoes. Miranda's mad about them. Ellis Martin was wearing a pair. A new, rather clean-looking pair. Hardly the sort of thing you'd wear for a walk in the woods. Particularly if you have a very serviceable, if trendy, pair of green wellies parked just inside your kitchen door."

"And did she?"

"Oh my, but yes."

"So she wasn't expecting to go walking in the woods?"

"I wouldn't have thought so," said Owen. "Especially not since it had been raining a bit and was rather damp. If she was planning to go for a walk, it wasn't a long one."

"Not, say, the distance between her house and Tinker Wood?"

"Exactly," said Owen. "So, one way or another, someone took her up there. And counting out the likelihood of a kidnapping murderer who is neither a sex fiend nor a robber, I think that we can safely assume that it almost had to have been someone she knew."

"And yet, if she knew that she was going to meet them, why wasn't it written down in her diary?"

"Either because she didn't know or she didn't want anyone else to find out."

"Correct," said Ross. "Which brings us back to something else that I don't like about all this. Why would Ellis Martin have wanted to meet with Kate Davidson that evening?"

"They were old friends? Ellis was getting married. Perhaps she wanted to make amends?"

"Does anything that we've heard so far lead you to believe that Ellis Martin was the sort of person who would care about making amends?"

"No," said Owen, "I'm afraid it doesn't."

"Unless, of course," said Ross, "she didn't make the appointment."

"The handwriting's hers," said Owen.

"No, no. I didn't mean that. I meant that perhaps Kate Davidson invited her."

"You're suggesting that Kate Davidson invited her up to The Hall on some pretext or other and bashed her on the head with one of David Grainger's spades when she arrived?"

"I don't know," mumbled Ross. "I don't know what I'm suggesting."

"There is, of course, the fact that Kate Davidson apparently did nothing at all about trying to find out about Ellis. If she did invite her, that's very odd. Very odd unless she knew perfectly well where Ellis was. Knew, in fact, that Ellis was dead. Either because she had killed her or—"

"Or she knew that someone else had."

"Do you really see David Grainger killing her?"

"I don't know what I see," said Ross. "But first thing tomorrow, while I'm at the inquest, I want you to confirm both Kate Davidson's and David Grainger's alibis. Start digging. Find people who saw Grainger that afternoon and evening. Find out exactly how Kate Davidson walked to and from The Snipe and find out if anyone saw her."

"And if not?" asked Owen.

"If not," said Ross, "we'll get forensics into The Hall and the outbuildings and all over Wildesham Place. It's almost ten days. But you never know, we might get lucky."

"Do you think they could have acted together?" asked Owen.

"I don't know," said Ross. "It's possible."

"Motive?"

"Rage, anger, pain, revenge. Desire for a sense of justice? Hate. As far as I know, those are the things that people usually kill for."

"Well, well, well," said Owen, "I wouldn't have bet on a crime of passion."

"So far it's nothing of the sort, nor anything else," said Ross. "And unless we get something, that's about where it's going to stay."

After Owen left, Ross sat in his uncomfortable chair and stared out of the window. It had been recently cleaned, not something that would ever be likely to happen in a London police station, he thought. Even in New Scotland Yard he could not remember seeing a shiny pane of glass outside of a laboratory. They clean the windows here, he told himself, because here in the countryside life is civilized and charming.

His ruminations on the charms of country life were interrupted by a tap on the door. Ross called out and a constable came into the office and placed a package carefully on the desk. Ross signed for it and the constable departed, closing the door carefully behind him. Ross sat for a moment and looked at the package. Then, very carefully, he opened it.

Inside the package was the scarf that had been placed over Ellis Martin's face before she was buried. Ross had requested that it be sent to him as soon as forensics had finished with it. He glanced at the lab report and then he pushed it aside and carefully spread the square of silk across his desk.

The earth from the grave had not left as many marks on the heavy silk as might be expected. Nor had Ellis Martin's blood. Only the top quarter, the part which would have draped down over the gash in the side of her head, was heavily stained. The rest was quite clean and the pattern was easily discernible. Ross felt a heavy sense of sadness as he looked at the familiar pattern of bright flowers and jungle leaves that surrounded the lion's face.

"Where did you get it, Billy?" asked Dierdre Carter, holding up the earring. Billy looked at his mother with growing discomfort. He recognized the look on her face. It meant that she was likely to go on and on and on until she got an answer to whatever it was that she wanted to know. Of course Billy Carter knew perfectly well that he should have given the earring to the police when they were searching up in Tinker Wood. But, on the other hand, he was the one who'd found it, wasn't he? And after all, Tinker Wood was his own personal preserve. He couldn't go about letting everyone know where his forts and hideouts and dugaways were. He knew that he should have kept that earring up in the wood with the rest of his special possessions. Instead he'd decided to bring it home and keep it in his treasure drawer in his room. He liked the blue stone in the middle and he'd bet anything that the metal around the edge was gold. It was loads better than anything any of the other boys had. Billy liked to get it out at night after he was supposed to be asleep and hold it up to the night-light in his room and see how it sparkled.

Now, however, his mother had got a hold of it. She'd probably found it when she was cleaning which was, Billy knew, just another name for spying on him. She liked to make sure that he didn't have any cigarettes or bubble gum or any of the hundreds of other things that she seemed to have on her black list.

"Billy," his mother said ominously. It was getting dangerously close to time for Top Of The Pops. She had him up against the wall.

"In the wood," Billy said sullenly.

"What wood?" asked his mother.

Billy jerked his head to the left. "You know," he said. "The wood, up there. Where the lady was done in."

Dierdre frowned and dropped the earring into her apron pocket. "Well, first thing tomorrow morning, when I go to do the shopping, it's going to the police, hear? It's probably valuable and that and I shouldn't be surprised if someone's lost it."

Billy scowled at his mother and was suddenly relieved that tomorrow was Tuesday and that there- fore he would be in school and unable to accompany her on the bus to Millbrook. He knew perfectly well that she'd make him apologize to the police for not giving the earring back right away. This murder, thought Billy, had been an awful lot of trouble. As far as he was concerned, life would be a lot simpler once everyone stopped messing about up in the wood and life got back to normal.

Ross was on his way home when the telephone call came through. The constable on desk duty caught him just as he was about to go out of the station door.

"Chief Inspector," he called, holding his hand over the mouthpiece of the telephone. "I've a call here. A Mr. Harry Matchum insists on speaking to you. He says it concerns Ellis Martin."

Ross nodded and went back down the hall to his office.

Harry Matchum's voice had the thick, slow burr of a Yorkshire accent. "Harry Matchum here, Mr. Ross," he said. "I'm ringing about Miss Ellis Martin. Terrible thing."

"Yes," said Ross. It crossed his mind that taking this call might have been a mistake.

"You see, Mr. Ross," Harry Matchum was saying, "I spoke to Miss Martin not three weeks ago." Matchum paused.

"Go on," Ross said. He had pushed the other extension button on his phone and as a result the duty constable from the front desk appeared in the doorway of his office.

"Lovely girl, Miss Martin," Harry Matchum said. "Or so she sounded. I never met her, strictly speaking. She contacted me by telephone."

Ross handed a slip of paper to the duty constable.

On it he had written the single word, "trace." He hoped they knew how to do that in Millbrook. Apparently they did since the constable glanced at it and disappeared back into the hallway.

"You see," Harry Matchum was saying, "I read about it in the paper and thought, here you are, Harry, chance to do the police a good turn."

"How did you know Ellis Martin?" Ross asked.

"It was odd really," Matchum replied. "You see, she contacted me, Chief Inspector. Wanted me to look into a matter concerning a Miss Clara Beale."

Ross felt himself stiffen with excitement. He sat down slowly and pulled his notepad toward him.

"Clara Beale?"

"That's right," Matchum said. "Old business, that, as far as news goes, but it was my story back then. Oh," he said laughing, "perhaps I neglected to mention, Mr. Ross, I'm a news hack with the *Scarborough Times*. The Clark Kent of the North, Chief Inspector, that's me. Harry Matchum's your man." He laughed again and Ross could hear him lighting a cigarette. "I suppose I'd better explain, really," Matchum said. "Don't suppose you big boys down at the Met would remember Briarcliffe."

"I'd be grateful, Mr. Matchum," said Ross. On his pad he printed the name "Briarcliffe." It meant nothing to him.

"Well," said Matchum, "Briarcliffe was my first big story. Loony bin up here. Real Brontë stuff, not one of your posh places if you get my meaning. Must be twenty years ago now. Stories started coming out about unpleasant goings on, patients getting rather more medication than they were meant to, and worse.

Then Clara Beale turned up dead. Story was that she'd gone out of control one night, fallen down stairs. Nasty accident. It probably wouldn't have caused much fuss, except that one of the orderlies had something verging on a guilty conscience. Spilled something to his sister and the sister started to talk. The autopsy on Clara Beale suggested something a wee bit more deliberate than a tumble down stairs. There was talk about hosing. Not a pretty story."

Ross shuddered. "And Ellis Martin contacted you about this?" Ross asked.

"That's right," Matchum said. "Said she had something to do with film. See, they did make one of those Beeb documentaries on it back then. Any road, Miss Martin called me, said she was doing something or other about it and wanted to hire me to look into it again. I don't mind doing a bit of that sort of thing and the remuneration was on the generous side. I did do a bit of digging for her and then, heigh ho, I pick up the *Telegraph* and there she is, dead as a doornail. Odd life, isn't it, Mr. Ross?"

"Yes," said Ross. "Yes it is."

"What I was wondering, Mr. Ross," said Matchum, "was if you wanted this stuff. I won't finish it off now, no point, is there? But what I've got's no bloody use to me, or to Miss Martin, for that matter. And she'd gone and paid me for it all as well, silly lass."

"I should very much like to see it," Ross said. "If you'll give me your numbers and address, I'll have the Yorkshire CID contact you, Mr. Matchum."

Harry Matchum obligingly turned over his telephone numbers and the addresses of his residence and "place of employ," as he quaintly put it.

"Anything to do The Bill a good turn, Mr. Ross," he

said, laughing. "Who knows, perhaps someday you'll have the pleasure of returning the favor?"

Ross found William DeWarre in the bar of the Cavendish House Hotel. He was sitting at a table beside the fireplace. There were papers spread out in front of him, but he didn't look like he was getting much work done. When he saw Ross coming across the room, he stood up and made a feeble attempt at smiling.

"Chief Inspector," he said as they shook hands, "will you join me?"

"That would be very pleasant," said Ross. He took his overcoat off while DeWarre went to the bar for a couple of scotch and sodas. When he came back he pushed the papers aside and set one of the glasses down in front of Ross.

"I was fooling myself that I might get some work done," DeWarre said, sitting down. There was a similarity between William DeWarre and David Grainger, not just physically, but in their manner. They were both kind men and both of them had the same sense of quietness. They were decent, thought Ross, gentlemen in the true sense of the word. He felt the familiar sadness rise within him, but this time the sadness was for Ellis Martin. She was lost, he thought, drifting on just too much money and perhaps just too much beauty to force her to live life as others did. She was reaching out for men like David Grainger and William DeWarre, reaching for something solid, something to hold on to. And equally he thought that she was hoping that someone would hold on to her, hold her down to life before she spun away. Some instinct of self-preservation worked in that lovely body, but perhaps did not work strong enough or soon enough to save her. Poor Ellis, he thought. It is always the lost children who wander one step too far and end up in places like Tinker Wood.

William DeWarre was watching him. Ross wondered if they had been in the same place. He raised his glass. "Good health," he said.

DeWarre raised his glass and smiled sadly.

"Amen," he said.

"Tell me," Ross asked, "what does the name Briarcliffe mean to you?"

"Briarcliffe?" DeWarre thought for a moment and then put his glass down. "Well," he said, "it was a mental institution, quite a notorious one, up in Yorkshire. A famous documentary was made about it. The place was closed down as the result of an official enquiry into brutality. It sparked pretty much a complete reform in public institutions of that type. Must have been twenty or thirty years ago."

"Why would Ellis have been interested in it?"

"Ellis?" He took another sip of his drink. "Well, we saw the film recently. The BFI owns a copy, of course. It was one of the ones we screened for this retrospective thing. But I don't know that it interested Ellis particularly."

"Apparently it did," said Ross. And then he told William DeWarre about his phone call from Harry Matchum.

When Ross had finished, DeWarre simply sat and stared at him for a moment. Then he said, "How extraordinary. So that's who Clara Beale is. Or rather, was."

"That's right," said Ross. "I haven't seen Matchum's report yet. But that is, apparently, who

Clara Beale was. What I'd like to know is what possible interest Ellis could have had in her."

"All I can think," said DeWarre, "is that it must have been a special project that she was working on for this course at Canterbury. I think I remember that she had to prepare some kind of special topic for research. I should think she fastened on the Briarcliffe film. It is quite sensational and it was very important. Yes," he said, "now that I think of it, that makes perfect sense."

Ross had to admit that he was right.

Chapter
9
•

Barry Glen was on duty at the Millbrook police station on Tuesday morning. He was actually a bit cheesed off about this. Tuesday was the morning of the inquest and all, and Barry had hoped that he might be called in to stand at the door and control potentially riotous crowds or hand things in plastic bags back and forth. He would have given anything to be able to describe the morning's goings on to Angie. But it was not to be. Here he was stuck on desk duty while high drama was being played out just a building away.

Barry was contemplating the injustice of life when the door opened and Dierdre Carter came in. He knew Dierdre in passing; her husband had a little house-painting business and Barry and Angie saw them occasionally in the pub.

Today Dierdre was looking annoyed and slightly harassed. Well, so would I, thought Barry, if I had a five-year-old and an eight-year-old.

"Hello, Dierdre," he said. "What can I do for you?"

"Well actually," Dierdre said, "I've come to return something. I mean turn something in, really."

"And what might that be?" he asked, wondering what on earth Dierdre Carter might be in possession of that needed to be turned in at a police station. She hardly looked like the type to be harboring illegal weapons.

Dierdre took a small white box out of her purse and set it down on the counter.

"I'm sorry," she said. "It's that wretched little Billy of mine. He found it, he says. Since I thought it might be valuable and all, well, I thought you'd best have it."

"I see," said Barry. He opened the box and looked at the earring that sat there. It was set in something that looked like gold and it had a blue stone in the middle. It was the type of earring that people with pierced ears wore. Barry and Angie had recently seen *Beau Geste* on television. If that stone was a sapphire, he thought, it certainly might be valuable. "Well, that's very good of you, Dierdre," he said. "If more people took a little responsibility, the world would be a better place." Dierdre made a clicking sound with her teeth, but she looked pleased all the same.

"Well, you know little boys, Constable," she said. "He didn't mean to do anything wrong, but they will pick things up."

"Yes indeed they will," Barry said. The two of them stood for a moment admiring the earring and their own greater sense of wisdom and responsibility in a world gone mad. "Now then, Dierdre," he said, picking up his pen and clearing his throat in a businesslike manner, "so as I can make out a report, where did you say Billy found this?"

"Well I didn't say," said Dierdre, "but he says he found it up in Tinker Wood."

The inquest had gone exactly as Ross expected. The evidence, what little there was, had been given in something like record time. The only possible verdict had been handed down by the coroner. Ellis Jane Martin had, on or about the afternoon of Friday, February fourth, been unlawfully killed by a person or persons unknown.

There hadn't been many people there: William DeWarre, Mrs. Jeffers, the shopkeeper's wife who last saw Ellis alive, Mary and Sam Jepp, and, somewhat to Ross's surprise, Kate Davidson. Now, as he stood on the pavement wondering whether or not he was hungry, he heard Kate calling his name.

She was dressed more conventionally today. In fact, she was nearly unrecognizable in a navy blue suit and expensive little dress shoes. Her hair, however, distinguished her. It was as unruly as usual and in the bright sunlight the brown in it had taken on distinctly reddish overtones. She was having trouble keeping it out of her eyes.

"Chief Inspector," she called as she came down the pavement toward him, "I was hoping to see you." She stood in front of him, smiling. "I feel as if I should ask you to call me Kate," she said, "but somehow I think you'd disapprove. There's something I wanted to tell you. Do you have a minute?"

"Of course," said Ross. "Won't you come to my office?" He had turned and started to lead the way to the police station when William DeWarre caught up with them.

"Chief Inspector," he said, "I'm sorry to bother you—"

"That's quite all right, Mr. DeWarre," said Ross. "I don't believe you know Kate Davidson? Miss Davidson, this is Mr. DeWarre, Ellis Martin's fiancé."

Ross wasn't sure whether he imagined it or whether Kate actually hesitated before putting her hand out to DeWarre and saying, "I'm so terribly sorry."

DeWarre shook her hand and thanked her before he turned back to Ross.

"I won't keep you, Chief Inspector," he said. "I just wanted you to know that I'll be going back up to town tomorrow morning. I wondered if I might have a moment of your time before I leave, say this afternoon?"

"Yes," said Ross, "that would be fine. Why don't I come to you? Say at two at the Cavendish?"

DeWarre nodded and, thanking him, turned away. Kate watched him as he threaded his way down the pavement. Ross thought, for a moment, that she was going to say something, but then she seemed to change her mind and allowed him to usher her through the main door of the police station.

Barry Glen was behind the desk when they came in. He was a nice enough young man, thought Ross, if a bit damp behind the ears. A girl stood at the desk. She was holding a shopping bag. She looked shyly at Ross and then stepped back into the lobby. Ross got the distinct impression that he had invaded a private conversation.

Now Barry was looking at him eagerly and Ross felt a twinge of guilt that he hadn't dreamed up some pretext for allowing him into the inquest. To make up for it, Ross said, "Unlawful killing, Constable. No surprise there for any of us."

"No, sir," Barry said, delighted at being allowed in on such information, hearing it straight from the horse's mouth, as it were, instead of third hand from the grapevine. Ross was about to continue on down the corridor to his office when Barry, taking his courage in both hands, said, "Chief Inspector? Excuse me—"

"Yes, Constable Glen, what is it?" asked Ross. Barry looked uncomfortably at Kate Davidson.

"I'll wait in your office," Kate said quickly. "Is it just here?"

"Yes," said Ross, nodding toward the open door. "Make yourself at home."

Barry Glen produced a small white box and placed it on the counter in front of Ross.

"I'm sorry, sir," he said, "but Detective Inspector Davies is still out. And, well, I thought you might want to see this right away."

"What is it?" asked Ross, taking the box.

"Well," said Barry, "it's an earring, sir. A lady's earring, sir," he added, "for a pierced ear. I believe it may be valuable, sir. But the thing is, it was turned in this morning by a woman named Dierdre Carter. And she says her son Billy found it while he was playing in Tinker Wood."

Ross opened the box and looked at the earring which lay there on a small piece of tissue paper.

"Did he now?" said Ross. "Well, well, Constable Glen, that is extremely helpful. Thank you." Barry Glen beamed with self-importance as Chief Inspector Ross dropped the box into his pocket and stepped into his office, closing the door behind him.

Kate Davidson was sitting in his visitor's chair going through her handbag. Ross went to his desk and, extracting an ashtray from his drawer, pushed it toward her. She looked up and shook her head.

"No thanks," she said. "I'm cutting back, or at least saving my awful habits for at home."

"What can I do for you, Miss Davidson?" Ross asked. He pushed his chair back against the wall and sat down. She finished playing with the contents of her bag and looked at him. A lock of hair fell across her face and she smiled as she pushed it away. Could this woman really be a murderer? Ross asked himself. Of course she could. Killers could wear charming little blue suits just as well as anyone else. Having pretty ankles did not, in so far as he knew, affect one's ability to hit someone in the head with a spade.

"Well," Kate said, "I don't know if this is important or not, but having had my wrist slapped once, I thought I'd better let you be the judge of that. You see, I've remembered something that Ellis told me, oh, it must be a month ago now."

"Go on," said Ross.

"It was about this planning business, you know, the haulage depot that's being built on the land adjoining mine? Or rather, my parents'," she added. Ross nodded and she continued. "When the plans first came to light there was a terrible foofaraw over it," Kate said. "Petitions went round and the whole thing. Everyone was terribly upset. When the plans were actually approved by the local council in spite of such strong local opposition, they were even more upset. As you can imagine, my parents were particularly horrified."

"Yes," said Ross, "I can quite well see why."

"Quite," said Kate. "In any case, they went to their solicitors and we tried to get a judicial review on grounds of improper procedure. In the end, there wasn't enough evidence, and the case was dropped. All that was about six months ago. Then, about a month ago, I saw Ellis in the village shop. As I told you, this planning thing and what's happening to the countryside round here, was something that both of us really did feel very strongly about. Anyway, I'd said hello to Ellis in the shop and when I left she followed me out and came over to the car. She said that she wanted me to know that she might have some good news about the depot. When I looked rather skeptical, she went on. She said that she might have found something that would stop it being built and would give Dawling, or 'that creep Dawling,' as she called him, a nasty shock. Dawling's the fellow who's building the bloody thing," Kate added. "He owns the garage in the village."

"And she didn't say anything about what this might be—this thing she'd found out?"

"No," Kate said. "Frankly, I assumed that it was nothing at all. Ellis was given to amateur dramatics. It kept her life from being dull. She was always saying the most horrible things about Dawling. Not that I don't agree with most of them. He's a rather horrible little man, but one doesn't want to be sued for slander. Anyway, I did ask her what she meant, but she went all coy on me. That was just like Ellis. She could be bloody annoying."

"And you've only just remembered this?" asked Ross.

"Well, yes and no," said Kate. "I suppose that I remembered it, but I attached no importance to it whatsoever. Ellis could be very silly. She'd gone around saying things about stopping the depot and fixing Dawling's wagon for ages. So had the rest of us at first. But when it became obvious that the damn thing was going to be built and we couldn't do anything about it, we had to get on with our lives. It's like ranting about the government. Everybody says they'd like to shoot them, but I don't know anyone who's bought a gun."

"Yes," said Ross.

"At any rate," said Kate, "I'd heard all this before, so I didn't pay any attention. And then, after talking to you, I started to wonder why it was that Ellis wanted to see me that night."

"And you think that perhaps Ellis was going to talk to you about what she'd found out about Mr. Drowning, or whatever his name is?"

"Dawling," said Kate, smiling. "Well, I don't know. Who knows what Ellis was ever going to do? But it did occur to me, yes. It's probably nothing at all. But you did say that everything about Ellis Martin was your business now."

"And so it is," said Ross.

After Kate had assured him that she could find her own way out, Ross took the small white cardboard box out of his pocket and placed it upon the desk in front of him. He looked at the earring for a moment, picking it up and turning it over in his hand. Then, quite suddenly, he dropped it back in the box, jumped up from his desk and hurried out of the office.

Kate Davidson was just about to start her car when she looked in the rearview mirror and saw the Chief Inspector galloping down the street toward her. His great long legs and his flapping dark jacket made him look like a children's illustration that she had once done that featured a friendly spider called Max. She had to fight the urge to giggle as she turned off the radio and put the window down.

"I'm sorry, Miss Davidson," Ross said, "but there was one more thing that I wanted to ask you."

"Yes?" said Kate.

"Could you tell me whether or not you have pierced ears?" She looked at him for a moment as if he might have gone off his head and then she laughed and said, "Yes, as a matter of fact, I do." Ross straightened up.

"Thank you, Miss Davidson," he said. "I'm sorry to have kept you."

Owen made a humming sound as he turned the earring over in his hand.

"The back's missing," he said.

"I'm sorry?" said Ross. He had been standing at the window staring at the parking lot.

"The back to the earring," said Owen very carefully, as if Ross were deaf. "The thing that holds it on. It's missing. I should think that means that whomever lost it was wearing it at the time."

"Possibly," said Ross.

"When was it found?"

Ross crossed the room and took his overcoat off the hanger.

"I don't know," he said. "That's what we're going to find out."

"No one's reported it missing?" asked Owen, standing up and dropping the earring back into its box.

"No," said Ross. "And that's a bit strange, isn't it? Not to have reported the loss of a sapphire earring set in gold?"

"So it's real?" asked Owen.

"Oh yes, it's real. Worth quite a bit, I should think," said Ross as he opened the door. "So I'd think it unlikely that someone hadn't noticed it missing, wouldn't you?"

"Yes," said Owen, following him out. "Almost as unlikely as wearing it to go for a stroll in Tinker Wood."

Chapter

10

At first Billy Carter had felt positively puffed up with pride at the idea that he was going to miss maths because he had to talk to the police. Now, however, as he sat in the head's office waiting for them, he wasn't at all sure that he liked the idea. Billy was beginning to wish that he'd never seen the wretched earring to start with. He was probably going to be arrested and thrown into Maidstone jail. Or he might be sent to one of those schools full of boys who'd done really awful things and who would eat him alive because he wasn't, after all, very big, even if he was almost seven and two-thirds. His mother was always telling him not to be a chatterbox, and in this case he was going to take her advice.

The policemen, when they arrived, were not quite what Billy had expected. For a start, neither of them wore a uniform. They didn't look much like Starsky and Hutch, either. One of them was very, very tall and the other was short and spoke with what Billy thought was a funny accent. Billy slouched further into his chair and wished that he was somewhere else.

"Hello, Billy," said the tall man. "I'm Chief Inspector Ross and this is Detective Inspector Davies." Billy nodded. The shorter man brought out the box that Billy's mother had put the earring in the night before. He took the lid off and Billy could see the earring sitting there on a piece of tissue paper.

"Is this the earring you found, Billy?" the short man asked. Billy nodded, wondering if any minute now they were going to march him off in chains or make him give up the whole three weeks' allowance that he'd been saving up to buy a set of felt tip pens.

"Could you tell us where you found the earring, Billy?" the tall man asked.

Billy sat up a little straighter. He liked the tall man. He was wearing a dark blue tie with a zigzag on it that looked like red lightning.

"I found it in Tinker Wood," Billy said. He started to add that that was where the lady had been found dead. Then he remembered about being a chatterbox and decided to leave that out.

"I see," the tall man was saying. "It was a very important thing that you found, Billy," he continued, "and it would be a great help to us if you could try to remember when it was that you found it."

"On the weekend," said Billy. "I play there on the weekend," he added.

"This last weekend?" the shorter man asked. Billy shook his head. This one was clearly a thicko. Didn't everyone know that last weekend the whole place was covered with police? As a result, Billy hadn't been allowed to go near the wood, much less play in it.

"No," said Billy. "Not last weekend, the one before." The two policemen looked at each other and Billy wondered if he'd said something wrong.

"Are you sure of that, Billy?" the shorter one asked. "Are you sure that it was the weekend before last and not some time earlier?"

It was Billy's greatest treasure to date and hardly the sort of thing that he was likely to make a mistake over. "I'm sure," he said.

"There's one more thing, Billy," the tall man said. "Do you think that you could do something for us? Do you think that you could come with us and show us exactly where it was in Tinker Wood that you found the earring?"

Billy looked from one policeman to the other. It seemed to him that by now they had probably made up their minds not to send him to a reform school, or even to Maidstone. He didn't much like the idea of anyone knowing exactly where his forts were in Tinker Wood. But then again, he wouldn't have to reveal those. He'd just have to show them where he'd found the earring, which was straightforward enough. Besides, a rapid calculation in his head confirmed that he would miss geography, which would be quite a good thing, since Billy had very little interest in remembering which was the longest river in Britain.

"All right," said Billy.

The tall policeman smiled and stood up. "Good fellow," he said. "Would it be all right with you if we went straightaway?"

Billy was rather disappointed that it was not actually a police car with a siren that he got to ride in, but it was a very big black car and he did get to sit in the front while the smaller man sat in the back. When they got to May Green the tall policeman asked Billy where they ought to park. Billy directed them up the lane toward The Snipe. He was feeling quite important by now and he led the two policemen onto the path that cut through the middle of Tinker Wood.

Ross and Owen followed the small boy without speaking. He was a strange child, thought Ross. There was something feral about him. As he picked his way carefully along the narrow, rutted footpath, he was following more or less the same route that Mary Jepp must have followed. Suddenly he veered off, turning into the undergrowth. At first Ross thought that he had merely cut into the wood, then he saw that there was, in fact, a child-sized gap in the brambles. This was clearly Billy's home ground and Ross felt like a large, clumsy giant as he pushed his way through the bushes and saplings. He could hear Owen behind him crunching through the dead leaves and branches.

A few moments later, Billy stopped. Ross came up beside him and saw that they were standing just above the drive to the abandoned cottage.

"Here?" Ross asked. The banks of brambles and bushes were thick along the edge of the old drive. Already they were starting to grow in on it, encroaching over the packed clay and mulch of leaves. Billy was so small that he was almost lost in this semi-wilderness and Ross could understand why it was that he came here to play. For a small child, this was an entire forest, a maze of trails and paths out of the eyes of the adult world.

Billy dropped to his hands and knees and a moment later he was standing in the drive to the cottage. There was a tunnel through the brambles, a child-size crawl space through what was, to someone of Billy's height, a solid wall of undergrowth. Now Billy called, "Here."

It took Ross and Owen a few minutes to make their way around the brambles and into the drive.

"Can you show me exactly where?" Ross asked. Billy nodded and stepped forward to the edge of the drive where the tangle of brambles met a bank of old leaves. He knelt down and placed his hand on the ground.

"Here," he said.

"Billy," Ross said, crouching down to meet the little boy's eyes, "that afternoon, when you found the earring, did you see anything else? Anything at all?" Billy looked at him solemnly before and then he shook his head.

"No," he responded.

"It could have belonged to Ellis," said Owen, "although there's no match to it in the house. If she was wearing them when she was killed, well, the other one's disappeared. She did have pierced ears. If our murderer noticed one missing, they could have removed the other."

"I'll see if DeWarre can identify it," said Ross.

"Kate Davidson—"

"Has pierced ears." Ross finished the sentence for him.

Suddenly he was tired of the whole investigation, tired of Ellis Martin. He decided that, whether or not she was dead, he thought that she was a boring, self-centered woman and he wondered if he was really the least bit interested in her at all. Maybe it was time to do what Kendal had talked about. After a few more years they'd planned that he should leave the police, start something else.

"Do something that will make you believe in the

better part of life," Kendal had said. Well, she was the better part of life and she was gone.

"What's bothering you, Master?" Owen asked.

He smiled and said, "Nothing. I'm hungry. Let's go and get something to eat."

"It could be nothing at all to do with the murder or the murderer," said Owen as they walked down the pavement. Ross was beginning to be sorry that he'd ever shown Owen the wretched earring. "It could simply have been dropped there some time ago," Owen continued. "It could be coincidence."

"I don't believe in coincidence," Ross said as he led the way into the George and Dragon.

They had finished most of their plowman's lunches when Ross finally said, "Right, tell me what you've got on David Grainger and Kate Davidson for the afternoon and evening of Friday, February fourth." Owen was cutting the last of his cheddar cheese into neat squares to match it up with his remaining chutney and bread. He shook his head.

"David Grainger was working on the farm, or so he says. One of the men saw him just after twelve in the farm offices. After that the men go home for lunch and they don't get back until about two. According to Grainger, he had a sandwich in the house and then went out to mend some fencing in one of the far fields. He says that he was out there until about half past three. One of the men who was stacking bales says he saw Grainger come back into the yard at what he thinks was about 4 P.M. He can't be sure. After that, Grainger was in the farm office until the men left at about six. Several people saw him. He says that that evening he went up to the pub in the village for a pint at about seven. That's confirmed by the landlord and a number of others. Apparently he was there until about eight or half past when he returned home and remained there."

"So," said Ross, "no one can fix an alibi on him from, say, half past twelve to about 4 P.M. and again from approximately half past eight onward that evening."

"That's right," said Owen. "And he claims that he didn't see anyone, either. So, he certainly had ample opportunity to get into Tinker Wood between half past twelve and 4:00 P.M., kill Ellis Martin, bury her, and get home again. The same is true of the evening."

"That is assuming," said Ross, "that Ellis Martin was killed in Tinker Wood. And if she was, how did she get herself there? No one saw her walking. If she drove there's the problem of returning her car. And if he collected her the chances are too good that someone would have seen them. So far, no one's said a word about seeing Ellis Martin at all on Friday afternoon, much less seeing her with David Grainger." He concluded, "David Grainger in the afternoon doesn't play. Even if she came to the house or he collected her while the men were at lunch, it's too much to believe that someone didn't notice her getting there."

"All right," said Owen. "Agreed that the afternoon is unlikely. What about the evening? He goes to the pub, stays until half past eight, drives to Ellis's, collects her for some reason, takes her back to the farm, or to the wood for that matter, kills her, buries her, et cetera, et cetera, et cetera."

"Then why didn't she go to Kate Davidson's at six?"

"She did and Kate's lying?"

"Why? It doesn't help either of them."

"Ellis changed her mind and didn't want to see Kate after all? Grainger rings her, says he'll collect her at eight-thirty and she decides to stay home and wash her hair? I don't know."

"Perhaps," said Ross. "But it doesn't make any particular sense."

"Well, not everything does," said Owen.

"All right," said Ross. "What about Kate Davidson?"

"Ah, well. Our lady painter was certainly seen by several people, the vicar among them, on her way to The Snipe. The footpath that she used runs through the churchyard. The vicar thinks it was about half past twelve when he saw her. He was on his way into the vicarage for lunch and he saw her coming up the hill. Apparently he waited for her and they walked some of the way together. That works out because she was seen by a lot of people in The Snipe from about 1 P.M. She says that she walked the long way to The Snipe, which means going around the back of Tinker Wood, in fact, across the back of the Grainger farm. All that's all right, incidentally, because the timing makes sense. Coming back is a bit different. She says that she walked from The Snipe down the lane toward May Green. Then she claims to have cut into Tinker Wood and followed the footpath through the bottom of the wood, which would be below the cottage and the old drive. That was at about three o'clock. She then cut across the fields and made for the old Roman road, which she says she followed up the valley and back to The Hall. She can't remember seeing anyone and, so far, no one reports seeing her."

"What about the evening?" asked Ross.

"Well," Owen said, "you know most of that. By the time she got home the daily was gone. She says she saw no one until the following day. She was at home all afternoon and all evening. Supposedly waiting for Ellis. According to her, that is."

Ross made a disgruntled humming noise.

"I don't like the afternoon for the same reason that you don't like it for Grainger," Owen said, lining his cheese squares up along the side of the plate. "Visibility. How Ellis got to and from, whether she was dead or alive at the time. But the evening is another thing. Kate could have made the arrangement with Ellis herself. She could have gone and collected her, brought her back to The Hall, bumped her off, taken her up to Tinker Wood, and buried her, just like that. Or she could have taken her straight to Tinker Wood and done it."

"The risk of being seen," said Ross. "Her car is even more visible than Ellis's."

"It's a risk," said Owen, "but it's possible. It was dark by six. People see Kate driving around all the time. They simply might not remember it. Or, no one saw her."

"It's possible," said Ross.

"It's very possible," said Owen.

"Motive?"

"Hatred. Pure and simple. And if Ellis was at The Hall or at Wildesham Place, we'll find something."

"All right," said Ross, "get a warrant and start. And try again. I want someone to have seen them driving about that night."

Owen smiled. "I think this calls for coffee," he said.

Ross was feeling uneasy. He had to admit that Owen was right. All of the facts were pointing in one direction. His instincts just didn't want to go along with them. He wondered why it was that he was so certain that William DeWarre would not be able to identify the earring as belonging to Ellis. Perhaps, he thought, he was just being stubborn or obtuse. Still, he had to admit that he hoped that they wouldn't find the mate to Billy Carter's earring in Kate Davidson's jewelry box. Perhaps he just liked David Grainger and thought that Kate Davidson had nice ankles. He reminded himself that Lizzie Borden probably had nice ankles too and that this was why you worked in pairs, to stop yourself being bloody narrow-minded.

The coffee arrived. He dropped two sugar lumps into the red cup and then poured the cream, watching it spread across the top of the dark surface in a thin, white swirl.

Chapter

11

No," said DeWarre. "No, I've never seen it before."
Ross nodded and put the earring back in its box. "Of
course," DeWarre added, "that doesn't mean that it
isn't Ellis's. But I don't think so."

They were alone in the sitting room of the Cavendish House Hotel. The fire had been lit and there were
fresh flowers on the center table. Even so, thought
Ross, the room felt empty and rather desolate. William DeWarre looked exhausted. His face was drawn
and slightly gray. Ross noticed that he was still unable
to bring himself to use the past tense. Grief is much
the same in everyone, he thought. We all think we're
different and yet the symptoms of our suffering don't
really differ much. There is the inability to concentrate, the forgetfulness over small things like eating
and where you put the car keys, the almost physical
revulsion at using the past tense. How long had it been
before he had been able to say, "it belonged to my

wife"? We go on fighting that fatal addition at the end of verbs that means, once and for all, that it's over.

"Mr. DeWarre," said Ross, leaning forward and resting his elbows on his knees, "I'm sorry to come back to this, but I'm afraid that I have to ask you again, is there anything, anything at all, that you can think of that was in any way unusual about Ellis's behavior in the last few weeks before you went to Spain?" DeWarre ran his hand through his hair and smiled.

"It's odd, isn't it, Chief Inspector," he said, "how difficult it is to really remember? I've thought and thought about it, of course. And now I can't quite sort out in my mind what was normal and what wasn't. Do you know what I mean? You're so used to someone and of course you don't know that they're going to, well, that something's going to happen to them, so you aren't watching for anything unusual. You aren't storing things up."

"I know," said Ross. "But anything, anything at all. Even if it seems inconsequential."

"We did what we always did, I suppose," said DeWarre. "Ellis was down here, mostly. She came up on the weekends. We went out to dinner. We saw friends. And then, oh, I suppose that it was about the week before I went away, something like that, Ellis came up for almost the whole week." He paused and went on. "It was the week before I went away. I remember because I was getting ready to go. I had to be at the office, at the BFI, quite late a few evenings. Ellis came to watch some film on a couple of nights, to pass the time until I was free to go to dinner."

"Was that unusual?"

DeWarre smiled. "No, not really. Except for the subject matter. Ellis was in her documentary stage just at that point. She became fascinated by Leni Riefenstahl." DeWarre looked at him, questioning. Ross shook his head. "Riefenstahl made films during the rise of the Third Reich. She was actually a ground breaker in her field. She made 'Olympiad,' among other things, about the Berlin Olympics, and really pioneered sports photography. Ellis was fascinated by her. She was particularly interested in 'Triumph of The Will.' That's a film that Riefenstahl made about the Nuremburg Rallies. It's really rather magnificent," DeWarre added, "if you don't mind the subject matter."

"I see," said Ross. "And that's what she was watching that week? Films by Riefenstahl?"

"Yes," said DeWarre. "But Ellis was like that. Once she decided that she was interested in something she could tend to go slightly overboard. In any case," he added, "I really can't think of anything. But if I do I shall certainly let you know. Thank you for sparing the time," he added. "I simply needed to know what was happening."

"Of course," said Ross. "We'll keep you informed. There is one more thing," he added. "I'm sorry about this. It may be rather unpleasant, but it is necessary." Ross waited for a moment while DeWarre looked at him. The expression on William DeWarre's face suggested that he could not conceive of things more unpleasant than those that had already occurred in the last week.

"Go ahead, Chief Inspector," he said.

Ross placed the scarf carefully on the coffee table in front of them.

"I'm sorry," he said, "but I have to ask you if you can identify this as having belonged to, or been in the possession of, Ellis Martin?"

William DeWarre sat perfectly still and stared at the bloodstained square of silk that lay spread on the table before him. It was not until he leaned forward and touched the deep brown stain, tracing its edge gently with his forefinger, that Ross realized that he was weeping. The tears ran in two straight columns down his cheeks and he made no attempt to wipe them away.

"No," he said softly, shaking his head. "No, I've never seen it before."

Outside a thin drizzle had started to fall. It was cold and for the first time in this unseasonably warm February it felt like winter. Ross looked at his watch. It was just past three. By now Owen should be moving into The Hall with a team from forensics. Ross felt a pang of conscience. He should, he supposed, have informed Kate Davidson himself of what was about to go on in her house. But one of the unfortunate things about this job seemed to be that violent death and civility rarely went hand in hand.

Ross came in the front drive of The Hall this time and parked in the courtyard beside Owen's Peugeot and one of the blue police forensics vans. The rain kept up and there was a sharp, blustery wind. He wondered, as he got out of the car and walked toward the house, why it was that the countryside always seemed colder. He had never remembered feeling the cold like this when he lived in London.

As he approached the front door it was opened for him by a policewoman. Owen, she informed him, was in the outbuildings. They had finished with the house an hour or so before. Ross thanked her and went back outside, following the path around the edge of the house. He found Owen in the garages.

Owen came toward him clapping his gloved hands together against the cold. Ross could read the disappointment on his face even from a distance.

"Nothing?" he asked. Owen shook his head.

"Not a damn thing. It's as clean as a whistle. Of course," he added, "that doesn't mean much. After all, there was a week to clean up in."

"Or it may not have happened here at all," said Ross.

"That's right. We're on to the car now and then we'll move down to Wildesham Place."

"Where is Miss Davidson?" asked Ross.

Owen nodded toward the house. "There," he said. "And I must say, she's as cool as a cat. Though I think she's none too pleased."

"I'll go and have a word with her," said Ross. Owen stood in the garage door and watched the tall thin figure disappear back around the edge of the house, his black overcoat flapping behind him.

Kate Davidson was in the same room where she and Ross had sat on Sunday. She had been reading, curled like a cat, as Owen said, in an armchair beside the windows. When Ross came in she put her book down and stood up.

"Chief Inspector." She didn't offer to shake hands, nor did she take off her glasses. They had thin gold wire rims that made her look more eccentric than usual. Ross closed the door behind him.

"May I have a word?" he asked.

"Please," she said. "Sit down."

Kate returned to the armchair. She waited for a

moment and then she looked straight at him and said, "I didn't kill her."

Ross sat down on the sofa and unbuttoned his overcoat.

"I last saw her on the Monday or Tuesday before she died," said Kate, "in the village. She never came here and I didn't kill her. I told you that."

"And I believe you," said Ross.

She continued to look at him and although her expression didn't alter he could sense the outrage that was pulsing through her. It came as something of a shock when he realized that she was angry with him. It wasn't the situation; it was him. He wondered for a moment if she was angry at his allowing this to happen or at the fact that he hadn't trusted her. He thought that it was likely to be the latter.

"Look, Kate," he said, "I honestly don't think that you killed Ellis Martin. But someone did and I think you can help me." She leaned back in her chair slightly.

"How?" she asked.

"You walked to The Snipe on Friday afternoon?"

"Yes."

"And how did you get there? By which route?"

"I went by the footpath, the way I always do."

"Which footpath?"

"I went down the valley from here and up the hill to the church. I went through the back of the church-yard—"

"Where you met the vicar?"

"That's right. And then I went along the top of the back fields, down the far side of the Grainger farm, and followed the perimeter of Tinker Wood around to The Snipe."

"And you didn't see anyone, other than the vicar?

You didn't, for instance, see anyone while you were on the Grainger farm?" She looked at him for a moment and then shook her head.

"No one."

"And how did you get back?"

"I walked down the lane from The Snipe and then I cut in on the bottom footpath that goes through the bottom edge of the wood."

"Below the old cottage and the drive?"

"That's right. And then I came out across May Green and followed the old Roman road up the valley and back here."

"I want you to think very carefully. When you were in Tinker Wood, on the way home, did you hear or see anything? Even sense anything? Anything at all?"

Kate thought for a moment. "I don't know," she said. "I've thought and thought. I just don't know."

"And you saw no one on your way home?" She shook her head. "What about cars? Did you see any cars on the May Green road? Any cars on the lane coming from The Snipe?"

"I don't know," she said. "Look, I'm sorry, but I can't be sure. I walk that path all the time, often exactly the same route. When I can't work, I often walk up to The Snipe for lunch. It's difficult to remember that day in particular. You see I would have remembered if I'd seen someone because that's so immediate. But cars are background things. I wasn't paying any special attention."

"I know," Ross said. She went on.

"I might have seen a car on the road or on the lane that day or it might have been the week before or two days after. I simply can't recall it that clearly." Ross leaned back on the sofa. Pushing her wasn't going to be any help at all. "I wish I could recall it completely," she said. "I wish I could be sure. But I can't."

"Kate," Ross said, "can you identify this?" He placed the scarf on the table in front of her. She stared at it and he watched the color drain from her face. She nodded.

"Yes," she said. "It's one of mine."

Ross leaned forward. "One of yours?"

She seemed unable to take her eyes off it. Without looking at him, she said, "I don't mean I own it. I mean that I designed it." She looked up at him and her eyes were filled with something like horror. "That's Ellis's blood, isn't it?" she asked.

"Yes," Ross said gently, "it is. Tell me about the scarves."

She got up and walked quickly across the room where she stood hugging herself as if from a draft.

"The scarves," she said. "I only started doing them last year. I was approached by a company called Persimmon, small but very high quality. I only did five designs for them and they do a limited run. Those sold quite well, so we were going to do more this year."

"Where are they sold?" Ross asked.

"Only two places. One's a trendy little boutique off Covent Garden called Persimmon, owned by the company. The other's Harvey Nichols."

"All right," Ross said. He stood up and buttoned his coat. "If you remember anything, anything at all—"

"I'll ring you immediately," she said.

"Thank you." He had started to open the door when she called him back.

"Chief Inspector?" She was standing in the middle of the room, the watery light catching her long, unruly tangle of hair. There was an earnestness in her voice that made him think of a child. "Chief Inspector," she said, "David Grainger didn't kill her either." Ross looked at her for a moment.

"No," he said. "I don't suppose that he did."

It was five o'clock on Wednesday evening before Owen finished with Wildesham Place. The results were no more spectacular than those from The Hall. The forensics teams had found nothing at all in either location. Owen sat in Ross's office nursing a cup of tea and relating what a waste of time it had all been. Ross was only slightly surprised to realize that what he felt was something like relief. He had never believed that Ellis had been killed at The Hall or at Wildesham Place. Had he been proved wrong it would have been a severe blow to his faith in instinct, not that he yet had any idea where she had been killed.

"It doesn't mean that one or both of them didn't do it," Owen said.

"No, it doesn't," Ross agreed. He placed the scarf on his desk and looked at Owen.

"'Cover her face. Mine eyes dazzle. For she died young.' Webster. Now there's a playwright for you," said Owen. "Forensics finished with that lot day before yesterday," he added. "Came up clean."

"Yes," Ross said. "Did you know that Kate Davidson designed it? Her work's very distinctive."

Owen stared at him. "Jesus Christ," he said. "How long have you known?"

"I suspected, but she confirmed it this afternoon. You're right," Ross added, "it's clean. No prints, nothing. As far as I'm concerned, however, it puts her out of the running as a suspect."

"Unless she's a bloody idiot or incredibly clever," said Owen. "But it's a bit of a risk for a double jeopardy, isn't it? Bit of a stretch to put it there herself and assume we'd think it was too obvious."

"Yes," said Ross, "I think that is a bit of a stretch. But it doesn't make things look good."

"You're not assuming that this is a coincidence? That Ellis just happened to be wearing a Kate Davidson scarf?"

"No," said Ross. "And William DeWarre couldn't identify it."

"It's rather distinctive," Owen said. "You'd think he'd remember it. So, our murderer's a lady wearing a distinctive scarf designed by a local painter and leaves it draped over the body? Or our murderer goes out of their way to implicate Miss Davidson, albeit in a fairly obvious manner? Number one: amazing coincidence. Number two: our killer's a moron. Number three: we're looking for someone who not only disliked Ellis Martin, but doesn't have much time for Kate Davidson either." Owen leaned forward and fingered the heavy silk. "So, what now, Master?" he asked.

"They're sold in only two places," Ross said, "Harvey Nichols and a boutique in Covent Garden called Persimmon. The company that makes them is also called Persimmon. They only made a limited number last year."

"Bob's Your Uncle," said Owen, standing up to leave. "We'll have someone on it first thing. And now," he added, "I'm fed up with this and I'm going home to my lovely wife before she files for divorce on the grounds of desertion."

"Give my best to Miranda," Ross said. "And Owen,

keep looking for someone who saw Ellis Martin in a car after twelve noon on the fourth. Keep on looking for that wretched girl who took the phone call from the school office. And two more things: I want to know what was in Ellis Martin's will, if she left one, and I want to know about David Grainger's farm workers."

"You mean who could have taken the spade?"

"Along with everything else about them, yes. Find out if any of them had any connection, and I mean any connection at all, with Ellis Martin."

After Owen left, Ross sat in his office until 6 P.M. when the phone rang. She was right on time.

"Eugenie Pauling, head secretary at Canterbury," she said briskly. "We did say 6 P.M., Chief Inspector?"

"We did, Mrs. Pauling. Thank you for being so prompt."

She snorted, as if any other idea were inconceivable. "Well, Chief Inspector," she said, "I've done as you asked and you're right, our special seminar film students did have to nominate their special research projects in advance. The girl in question, Ellis Martin, had elected to do work on a documentary filmmaker called Leni Riefenstahl. A German," Mrs. Pauling added.

Ross felt a pang of disappointment followed by a small surge of excitement.

"There were no others, Mrs. Pauling?" he asked. "I mean the students didn't nominate a second subject or topic at all?"

"In the space of a week?" Mrs. Pauling laughed at the idea. "Good Lord, Chief Inspector," she said, "we're not utter slave drivers. No, they had only one topic and Ellis Martin's was Leni Riefenstahl."

Chapter

12

.

When he left the station, Ross had intended to go straight home. He wanted time to think about Ellis Martin away from the sounds of typing and telephone answering that were the continual background noise in the small, crowded station. It was not until he was driving through Wildesham that he realized that he was not following the most direct route toward his own home on the coast. Instead he was following the road that would lead him past Sam and Mary Jepp's house. He supposed that that was where he had been intending to go all along.

Mary Jepp made two neat slices through the lemon and dropped one into each gin and tonic. She handed one of the glasses to Ross and he followed her into the sitting room. Dog was already lying in front of the fire and he thumped his tail at Ross before settling down again to watch the flames.

"Sam'll be home shortly," Mary said, pushing some

newspapers off a footstool before she sat down. "I'm glad you dropped by," she added. "I really hate this time of day. It always seems so empty and depressing since the twins went off to school."

"I didn't come by for anything special," said Ross. "To tell you the truth, I was on my way home and I happened to be passing." Mary raised her glass.

"That's the best reason of all," she said. "Cheers."

"Cheers," said Ross. "Though, as a matter of fact," he continued after putting his drink down on the carefully placed coaster, "there was something, Mrs. Jepp, that I would like to ask you about."

"Yes," said Mary, "I thought there might be. I should think you'd better call me Mary, if you're going to keep coming around here and asking about Ellis." Ross smiled.

"Thank you," he said. "As a matter of fact, it wasn't so much about Ellis in particular as about the village."

"Oh?"

"Yes. I wondered if you could tell me about the haulage depot, the one being built on the land adjoining The Hall?"

"Oh, yes," Mary said. "The haulage depot. Well, as a matter of fact, I probably can tell you something about that. But then again, so can the rest of the village. There's been quite a fuss about it, one way and another."

"Tell me," said Ross.

She took a sip of her drink and swirled the ice around with her finger. "It's like this," she said. "The depot's being built by a man called Dawling. He lives here in the village and I'm afraid that he's not terribly well loved at the best of times. He owns a little transport company at the moment. You may have seen it. His garage is just outside the village. In fact, it's quite near Ellis's house. It's very small, nothing spectacular, just a few small lorries that used to do transport contracting for some of the local farmers. The apple growers mostly and, I suppose, some of the others. In any case, about a year ago a rumor started going around that he'd bought a piece of land on the farm that adjoins The Hall and that he was applying for planning permission to put a proper haulage depot up there."

"Bigger than the one he has now?" asked Ross.

"Oh yes," Mary said. "The story was that he had real dreams of glory. He was going to build this depot, a proper one with garages for maintaining lorries and the whole lot, and buy up more lorries and count on the fact that when the Channel Tunnel goes through he'd be in a wonderful position to make millions."

"And?" asked Ross.

"Well, for a start," said Mary, "no one could find out whether or not he'd actually bought the land. And then none of the neighboring landowners had been served with a notice that he'd applied for permission to put this thing up. Of course, we found out later that, strictly speaking, under the law, the council doesn't have to alert anyone. You know, send out notices. It's only supposed to. Well, it didn't and that got everyone's back up. It made them feel that there was something, I don't know, sneaky, going on."

"Not neighborly," said Ross.

"No," said Mary, "somehow not in the spirit of things. Well, in any case, we got wind of it and Kate Davidson went over to the planning office to have a look at the plans. She was horrified. They were pretty horrific. Garages, depots, the whole lot. So Kate started circulating a petition and got a letter writing campaign going. You see, this land is all officially green belt and designated solely for agricultural use. So we were all fairly certain that there was no way Dawling would get planning permission in the first place, but one wants to be certain. Kate even got her solicitors to send a planning consultant down and they got a hold of the road safety people. In recent years two people have already been killed on that road. It's the hills either way with the corners at the top. It's absolutely lethal. You can imagine what it would be like with bloody great lorries pulling in and out of there right off the side of the hill."

Ross had a brief recollection of his own near smash. "Yes I can," he said.

"So," Mary went on, "the road safety people came out to see it and said that, yes, indeed, although it was technically just within the bounds of the safety outlines, it would be lethal and that they intended to advise strongly against granting permission when they submitted their report. We were also concerned about having bloody great lorries rolling in and out through the village the whole time."

"What happened next?" asked Ross.

"Well, the first thing that happened was that Kate did a fabulous job getting this petition going. Every single family who lives on that side of the village signed it, and a lot of others besides. Hundreds of people wrote letters to the parish council and to the local councillor who sat on the planning board, Laura Ramsay. Dawling, in turn, got wind of that and took it as a personal affront. I believe he even threatened Kate."

"Threatened Kate?"

"Yes, the idea's actually rather ridiculous, isn't it?" Mary smiled. "But he's that sort of man, quite hysterical. Apparently he accosted her in the village shop and told her to stop trying to blackmail him. Said that her 'mafia-style American tactics' wouldn't work here and that she'd better go on back to the States where she came from."

"Dear me," said Ross.

"Quite," said Mary. "Actually, Kate thought that it was pretty funny and so did everyone else. If you saw Dawling you'd know what I mean. He looks slightly like a demented dwarf. In the end, everyone's mind was put at rest because when the vote went to the parish council, as it does to start with, they voted unanimously against it. Since parish council recommendations are almost never overturned, we were all virtually certain that that was the end of it." She picked up her glass and took another sip. "We were wrong. We all went along to the planning committee meeting, just for the sake of it. And, if you can believe it, they disregarded the parish council, disregarded the road safety report, disregarded the fact that the land is supposed to be for agricultural use only, and passed the damn thing! Gave him planning permission for a bloody haulage depot on the outskirts of a tiny, beautiful village like this!" Mary put her glass down and smiled. "I must confess," she said, "that that particular evening I wouldn't have missed stringing Laura Ramsay up by her ears from the rafters, if anyone had suggested it. You could have had a homicide on your hands much earlier than you did, Inspector."

"Why Laura Ramsay in particular?" asked Ross.

"She was our local councillor at the time," said

Mary. "She lives in the village and, everyone thought, was a relatively civilized, intelligent woman, even if she is a Conservative. When the letter writing business and the petitioning were going on, dear Mrs. Ramsay swore on bended knee that she'd vote against giving planning permission. Well, in the meeting, there in front of all of us, not only did she vote for it, she actually argued for it. Thatcher Toryism before your very eyes. In fact, we probably have Laura Ramsay to thank for the bloody thing as much as the wretched Dawling. She made a lot of people really furious. The upshot is that we have the depot and she can't get together a reasonable four for bridge anymore because no one's speaking to her, which is what she deserves. Here's Sam," added Mary, getting up. Ross started to rise but she took his glass and said, "No, stay. Let me get you the other half."

Ross wasn't in much of a mood to protest and in a moment Sam Jepp had joined them in front of the fire.

"I was just telling the Inspector about the depot drama and the perfidious Laura Ramsay," Mary said, settling herself on the footstool.

"Oh yes, Lady Ramsay," said Sam.

"There's a rumor abroad that Laura's of noble descent," said Mary, grinning.

"Shame it's not true, actually," said Sam. "It would keep her out of the Commons. Mary didn't enlighten you? Laura's the Conservative candidate in the upcoming by-election. All her dreams of power and glory came a step closer when poor old Aury Blaire dropped dead last month. In fact, it's a done thing."

"Yes," said Mary, "fortuitous that she backed the depot wasn't it? I'm sure that didn't hurt when they came to choosing a good new Thatcherite to inflict on us."

"Yes," said Sam, "I'm sure Laura will go far and do well. She's rather obnoxious, extremely ambitious, and terribly capable. And I do mean 'terribly.' She is also going to be our next area MP unless something very peculiar happens."

"Oh, God help us," said Mary.

"Tell me," asked Ross, "what happened after the planning permission was granted?"

"As far as the depot was concerned, nothing," said Mary. "It was in and that was that. Kate helped to found a village organization that's supposed to work as a watchdog committee on planning matters to stop something like this happening again. You know, in case we decide to apply to put a fast breeder reactor in the back garden, and there was an awful lot of hot talk, but there was really nothing that anyone could do."

"Katie tried, bless her," said Sam. "Her family even instructed their solicitors to engage counsel to try to bring a judicial review to look into the whole thing, but they couldn't find grounds."

"Were there any grounds?" asked Ross.

"Well, it was very odd, really," said Sam, "that the planning committee, or whatever they're called, should simply override the parish council, the road safety report, and strong negative local opinion. But that was probably as much due to Laura's persuasion as anything else. And she, of course, has her eye on bigger fish. It's a feather in her cap to have promoted some nice, booming local industry, what with the tunnel going through and the general Tory disregard for anything but profit at all cost."

"Tell me," asked Ross, "do you know if it's something that Ellis felt strongly about?"

"Yes," said Mary, "as a matter of fact, she did. Don't you remember, Sam? That night that we had the dinner party?"

"Oh, yes," said Sam.

"We had a dinner party," said Mary, "just after the permission was granted. Ellis happened to be down and we invited her. There were some other friends of ours from town who were staying. We started talking about the depot and Ellis got quite worked up. She was really furious about it, about what it would do to the area and that some little 'rat man,' as she called Dawling, could get away with doing such a horrible thing. There was even some speculation as to how he managed it."

Ross sat forward in his chair. "What do you mean?" he asked.

"Really, I think that that was the wine talking," said Sam. "But Ellis was speculating on the fact that there was something not quite right about the whole thing, about the way the voting went in the planning committee."

"Payola," said Mary.

"Ellis was fond of speculation," said Sam, "and the idea is fairly ridiculous. I don't honestly see Dawling paying off the planning committee any more than I see any of them accepting it. And besides, if there had been anything amounting to a whiff of suspicion, Kate's solicitor would have found out about it when they were getting ready to bring the case."

"Yes, you're right," said Mary. "It's just wishful thinking, but bribery was a nice idea."

Chapter

13
.

The garage was on the west side of the village. Ross was surprised to see that its perimeter fence formed the boundary to the gardens of a row of cottages on one side and a small wood on the other. Owen and Ross arrived in separate cars.

"I'm not surprised the planning committee wanted it out of here," said Owen as he got out of his car. "It's right in the middle of the bloody village." He slammed the door for emphasis. Owen was in a fit of bad temper and Ross was determined to ignore it. He was disinclined to indulge this Celtic flair for drama more than was strictly necessary. Owen was intensely annoyed at having been pulled off of his enquiries into David Grainger in order to go on some wild goose chase involving a haulage depot and petty council corruption. He had wasted no time in letting Ross know that he thought the whole idea half-witted.

Now that they had actually arrived at Dawling's garage, Ross had to admit that there was clearly good reason for giving permission for Dawling's business to move. At the moment the entire operation was almost in the village. Not that this amounted to much. There were several shed-like buildings that had a couple of lorries each in them. A pair of pumps, one for petrol and one for diesel, stood at the side of the yard. On the far side of the yard there was a low building with a sign hung over the door that read, Dawling Haulage.

The ambience was not one of prosperity, a fact which Ross found interesting in itself. How, on earth, did he manage to pay for the new site? He had to admit that, as far as appearances went, Sam Jepp was right. Looking at this place, the idea of Dawling having the cash to bribe anyone was pretty unlikely. Still, you couldn't judge by appearances. Perhaps Dawling was the type who kept it in shoe boxes under the bed.

Ross's musings on the state of Dawling's finances were interrupted by the appearance of the man himself. Ross now understood what it was that Mary Jepp had found funny in the idea of a potential threat to Kate Davidson's well-being. The man coming across the yard toward them was short and slightly rotund. He wore a tweed suit in a rather loud check that gave him the appearance of a cartoon character. His head and face were quite round and his springy, curling hair made him look slightly childish, despite the fact that it was going gray. A pair of round-lensed wire spectacles perched on the end of his nose. His potentially jolly appearance proved an illusion the moment he opened his mouth.

"I say there," Dawling shouted, "what do you want? This is private property!" The approach was unfortunate, given the already testy state of Owen's temper.

"Police," Owen said, snapping his identity wallet open in front of Dawling's nose. "Detective Inspector Davies and Chief Inspector Ross. Do I have the pleasure of addressing Mr. Kenneth Dawling?"

Dawling stopped dead in his tracks and looked from one man to the other. For a moment Ross wondered whether he was going to refuse to speak to them, which would be very tiresome indeed. Instead, Dawling became charm itself, something that Ross knew full well would only irritate Owen further.

"Gentlemen," said Dawling, positively beaming with pleasure, "please forgive me. We've had rather a lot of trouble lately with intruders, you know, village lads." Ross wondered if it wasn't time to get up to Huntsman for a new overcoat if he was being mistaken for a "village lad." He also wondered how many of the local vandals turned up in broad daylight driving Peugeots or BMWs. "Please forgive me," Dawling continued, his smile of welcome growing broader by the minute, "how may I be of service?"

Owen put his identity wallet back in his suit pocket and looked Dawling up and down with barely concealed distaste. Then he said, for what seemed like the hundredth time since Saturday, "We'd like to ask you some questions, sir, about Ellis Martin."

If Dawling was surprised by this announcement, he managed to conceal it. Instead he smiled and said, "Please, will you step into my office?"

Once they were seated and had refused coffee, Dawling leaned back in his office chair and, doing a competent, if heavy-handed, imitation of a visiting head of state granting an unpleasant interview, said, "Really, gentlemen, I can't imagine how I can possibly help you."

"Did you know Ellis Martin?" Ross asked.

Dawling nodded, but said, "Yes and no." He grinned. "If you get my meaning," he added. Ross thought for a horrible moment that he was going to wink at them.

"I don't, actually," said Owen, waspishly. "Could you be more explicit?"

"Well," said Dawling, ignoring Owen and addressing Ross in the spirit of one leader to another, "I knew *of* her, of course. You know what villages are like, Inspector. One big happy family."

One big happy family where one sibling's gone and bashed the other over the head with a spade, thought Ross. He could feel Owen's dislike of this tiresome man seeping across to him.

"Mr. Dawling," Ross said, leaning forward, "do I take it to mean that you did know Miss Martin personally?"

"Well, yes and no," said Dawling. It was obviously one of his favorite phrases but this time he had decided that it would be in his best interest to enlarge on it. "You can't live in a place like this and not know *of* almost everyone. But she was not a close acquaintance, so to speak."

"Did she have her car serviced here?" Owen asked. Dawling laughed at the very idea.

"Good heavens, Inspector," he said, "we haven't done that sort of thing in years. We only deal in transport," he added rather grandly.

"Could you tell me when you last saw Ellis Martin?" Ross asked.

After making a great show of furrowing his brow, Dawling replied. "No," he said. "It must have been some time ago, but I can't remember exactly."

"Surely you came in contact with her during the time when you were trying to obtain planning permission for the new depot?" Ross asked. He had been looking for a raw nerve and he had found it. This time Dawling had slightly more difficulty containing himself.

"No," he replied shortly.

"Ah," said Ross slowly. "I was given to understand that Ellis Martin was one of the people who particularly objected to the plans for the new depot. I wondered if, perhaps, she'd had reason to speak to you about it?"

"No," said Dawling, shaking his head emphatically.

"So you never spoke with Ellis Martin concerning the planning issue at all?" asked Ross.

Dawling's face was turning a rather unbecoming shade of red and Ross wondered if they were going to be treated to one of the displays of hysterics that Mary Jepp had described.

"There are a lot of people in this village," said Dawling, "who will do anything to stop progress of any kind. And there are those who have no compassion for other members of the human race, Inspector. They don't like to see anyone else get a slice of the pie. And there are some who have no business being here at all!" He was gathering force like a small tweedy tornado. "It was a sad day for England," he continued, "when just anyone could come and live here as they liked! I'll tell you that. And if you want to know something else," he added, "I'll tell you that you might be spending your time more profitably inquiring into how it is that some foreign nationals can live here and think that they run things just because America owns NATO!" Dawling added this last statement with a burst of patriotic fervor and sat looking at Ross as if he expected him to leap up and rush out to arrest Kate Davidson on a charge of cultural imperialism. Ross could almost hear "Rule Britannia" flooding through the dingy little office. He got slowly to his feet.

"Thank you for your time, Mr. Dawling," he said. "You've been most helpful."

Outside, in the parking area of Dawling Haulage, Owen announced that he had urgent matters to attend to and departed rapidly. The Peugeot spat gravel into the weed-filled ditch as he accelerated out of the drive. Ross got slowly into his own car. He left the Dawling garages and had just passed Ellis Martin's house when he noticed the sign. It read "Laurel House" and the discreet black lettering was glossy against the slightly off-white background. It was the last house before the crossroads into Wildesham. The garden beyond the neat split-rail fencing swept backward and disappeared behind a neatly clipped hedge. Doubtless a tennis court lurked beyond. Not, thought Ross, a new, rubbery, green-topped one, but an old red clay court, perhaps accompanied by a small pavilion with white beveled columns. The whole thing reminded him powerfully of "Mrs. Miniver," although he doubted that the lady of the house would be much like Greer Garson.

Almost without realizing what he was doing, Ross turned into the neatly graveled driveway. He supposed that it was curiosity as much as anything else that led him to pay this visit to Laura Ramsay. But that, he thought as he parked his car, was one of the great advantages of being a Chief Inspector. Satisfying his curiosity was part of his job.

Ross parked beside a new blue Volvo Estate assuming this meant that Mrs. Ramsay was at home. He rang the polished brass bell and waited. The woman who opened the door was more or less what he had expected. A composite portrait of a headmistress from the better type of girl's school, she wore tweed and cashmere and the pearls that had doubtless been presented at some long-ago twenty-first birthday and would also have graced her wedding portrait. He had been right also in suspecting that it was here that the spirit of Mrs. Miniver came to a halt. This woman bore a disturbing resemblance, not to Greer Garson, but to Margaret Thatcher and Ross remembered what Sam Jepp had said about her ambitions in the direction of Westminster. He had seen her before. This was the lady who had taken charge of the bicycle accident at the crossroads. He introduced himself and was shown into the sitting room.

A large brass bowl of very early daffodils sat on the coffee table and the sound of vacuuming came from the next room.

"Coffee, Chief Inspector?" Laura Ramsay asked.

"Thank you," said Ross.

"Please sit down." She waved him into an armchair and disappeared back into the hall. He heard her calling someone and shortly thereafter the sound of the vacuum stopped. When she came back into the sitting room she was accompanied by a Jack Russell terrier who climbed onto a footstool and regarded Ross solemnly.

"The coffee will be with us directly," Laura Ramsay said, sitting down. "What can I do to help you, Chief Inspector?"

"As you may be aware, Mrs. Ramsay," Ross said, "I

am leading the investigation into the death of Ellis Martin." Laura Ramsay nodded.

"Murder," she said. Ross looked at her. There was something slightly startling in the very definite way that she had made the pronouncement. Now she regarded him sternly. "The girl was murdered, was she not?" It was a statement rather than a question. "This was no ordinary death."

"That is correct," Ross said quietly. The impression that he was being interviewed rather than vice versa was reinforced. He was beginning to feel like a victim of Prime Minister's question time.

"Yes," Mrs. Ramsay continued, "a very tragic thing. But it's as well to get one's definitions right from the start, don't you agree, Chief Inspector? Ah," she added, "here is the coffee."

The coffee was brought in on a tray by a rather pretty blond girl who struck Ross as being slightly familiar. She smiled and withdrew as silently as she had come. Laura Ramsay turned to the business of pouring. The vacuuming had not been resumed and in the silence Ross could hear a grandfather clock ticking. The room smelled of furniture polish and daffodils. Mrs. Ramsay handed him a cup and saucer and sat back in her chair and smiled.

"You were talking about Ellis Martin," she said. Ross put his coffee down on the table.

"Did you know her?"

"Yes," Laura Ramsay said. "Not frightfully well. I had also known her aunt, Jane Martin. Or rather, my husband knew her. His family comes from the area," she added.

"I see," said Ross.

"Ellis was a nice girl," Mrs. Ramsay continued. "It

really is the most terrible thing. She came from a very old family, you know," she added, as if this should, at the very least, double the horror of being murdered.

"Do you know anything about the family?" Ross asked. Laura Ramsay placed her cup carefully back on the tray.

"Not really," she said. "I'm not altogether certain that there's that much to know. You would really have to ask my husband. You see, Ellis's parents were killed in an accident when she was a child. A most ill-fated family. Jane Martin was Ellis's father's sister. She became Ellis's guardian. I don't actually think that there was any more family. Jane never married."

"I see," said Ross. "And you didn't know Ellis herself?" Mrs. Ramsay smiled.

"You know how young people are, Chief Inspector. They hardly care to spend a lot of time with their parents' generation. I think, however, that we probably had Ellis here to drinks several times over the last few years. In fact, I'm quite certain that we did when she was engaged to David Grainger. David's father and mother were old friends. And I'm certain that she came to our New Year's Day drinks party just a month or so ago with her new fiancé. But I can't say that I knew her well. She seemed a most pleasant and capable girl. And, of course, very pretty, which is such a help for girls, isn't it?"

Ross nodded vaguely and decided not to mention that the only time he'd laid eyes on Ellis Martin she wasn't looking her best. Instead he said, "I understand that she was very concerned about the building of the new haulage depot?" Mrs. Ramsay laughed, displaying a perfect set of very healthy-looking white teeth. It occurred to Ross that she must once have been very pretty herself. Or perhaps handsome would be a better choice of word, like a well-bred horse.

"Chief Inspector," Mrs. Ramsay was saying, "almost everyone in this village has been concerned with the haulage depot, in one way or another. It has become something of a cause célèbre, at least it was last year. Not an awful lot goes on down in this quiet bit of the world, you know."

"But it was something that Ellis was particularly interested in?"

"It may well have been, yes. As I say, a lot of people were very worked up about it. But you may be confusing her with another young lady, Kate Davidson from The Hall. They were childhood friends, I believe." Ross was tempted to point out that this didn't make them in any way physically similar and that he would have to be blind to actually confuse the two women.

He resisted the temptation, perhaps from a childhood fear of having his knuckles rapped, and asked, "Ellis never came to see you, to speak to you concerning the haulage depot?" Mrs. Ramsay looked genuinely puzzled by the suggestion.

"No, Chief Inspector," she said. "Is there any reason that she should have?"

Ross felt vaguely silly now. This line of enquiry had come to a halt and he was sorry that he had taken up so much of this good county lady's time. He was tempted to ask her why it was that she had voted for the depot at all, but even he was beginning to have trouble seeing what on earth that could possibly have to do with Ellis Martin's death. He stood up and shook her hand.

"Thank you for your time, Mrs. Ramsay," he said.

She led him out into the front hall. There was a sideboard whose highly waxed surface reflected another bowl of daffodils. A rather fine watercolor hung above it and an oar painted in University colors was mounted along the length of the wall. Ross could just see the lettering that would spell the names of those who had been head of the river in some English summer long ago. She was holding the door open for him.

"Thank you again, Mrs. Ramsay," he said.

"Not at all, Chief Inspector," she replied. "Please let us know if there's anything further we can do." As the door closed behind him, Ross was sure that he could hear the Hoover starting up in the sitting room.

Chapter

14

The scarves," said Owen, "were in a limited edition of five hundred. Two hundred and fifty of them went to Persimmon and two hundred and fifty of them went to Harvey Nicks. They retail for £100 a piece, which my dear wife tells me is not unreasonable. If she didn't earn more money than I do, I'd take her flipping credit card away. In any case," he continued, "they went into stock in both stores on November fifteenth of last year. Persimmon sold out just before Christmas. Harvey Nichols still has three in stock. Both stores had fifty of each pattern. There is no way to trace which scarf was sold where. I've gone through Ellis Martin's financial records, Barclaycard, Access, AmEx, checks, the lot. There's no record of a purchase from Persimmon at all and nothing over £50 from Harvey Nichols. The only one I couldn't get was the last Access bill."

"So," Ross said, making a steeple with his fingertips, "either she put it on Access in the last month or she paid cash for it previously or it wasn't hers."

"Unless she was given it, stole it, or borrowed it, that is correct," said Owen. "However," he added, "you should be aware that the production manager at Persimmon, a spike-haired young lady called Grace, absolutely assured me that Kate Davidson was sent at least two scarves of every pattern during the production run."

"I see," said Ross.

"Yes," said Owen, "I thought you might. It makes you wonder, doesn't it, since she had more than one of each, how she could be quite so certain that the one you showed her wasn't hers?" The silence in the small office hung between them. "Look," Owen finally said, "I know you don't want to, but you've got to admit it." He leaned forward in his chair. "They both have a motive and neither of them has an alibi that's exactly cast iron. Either David Grainger or Kate Davidson or both of them could have killed Ellis Martin in Tinker Wood on the afternoon of February fourth. If they were in it together it would have had to have been between half past two and four P.M. On the other hand, either or both of them could also have killed her on the evening of the fourth, either in Tinker Wood or somewhere else."

"It is possible," said Ross.

"Thank you," said Owen.

"But I don't like it," Ross went on. "You've got almost nothing—"

Owen interrupted him. "I have opportunity in the afternoon and the evening. I have a murder weapon from Grainger's farm. There is a strong possibility that I have physical evidence and I have motive."

"Do you?" asked Ross.

"Yes, damn it!" Owen was getting increasingly annoyed with Ross's reluctance to be enthusiastic.

"What?" asked Ross.

"On Davidson's part, hatred and revenge. That's fairly obvious."

"And what about Grainger?" Owen shrugged.

"The same," he said. "Along with hurt and anger thrown in. He was the one who told us that he'd pleaded with her to have the child."

"Does he strike you as the sort of man who would hate like that?" Owen thought for a moment.

"You can't tell, but I will concede that she's the more likely of the two." Ross thought of the anger in Kate's face the last time he had seen her, the tensed sense of outrage, of a trust betrayed, that had emanated from her entire being.

"Yes," he said, "I'm quite certain that she is capable of that sort of emotion."

"And of acting on it," said Owen.

"Simply because people are capable of an action does not mean that they do it," Ross said, sounding to himself like a tired and over-used Confucius. Owen rolled his eyes. "I'm sorry," said Ross. "Are you thinking of them together or just one of them?" He didn't need to ask which one it would be.

"I'm not sure," Owen said. "I know it's not perfect. But that's what I've got and at the moment it's all we've got. I admit we need more physical evidence, but if they did it, I'll find it. And I'll also find someone who can place Ellis in or on her way to Tinker Wood that afternoon or evening."

"If they did it." Owen nodded.

"That's right," he said. "If. But if not, what the Hell

else have we got to go on? Some story that Kate Davidson made up about Ellis having something on that Dawling creature?"

Ross had to admit that it sounded rather farfetched. Sam Jepp was probably going to be right. And so was Owen. If Kate had killed Ellis then the story was rather a feeble smokescreen. And that in itself seemed almost as unlikely as being stupid enough to lay your own scarf over the face of someone you'd just murdered. Surely someone with Kate's brains could come up with something better than that? And why not, after all, stick to the original premise that she had no idea why Ellis wanted to see her? Why come to Ross two days later with something as bizarre as a story about Ellis being an amateur sleuth? Ross thought that Kate was probably telling the truth, that, in fact, Ellis had said something to her. After all, she had said the same thing at the Jepps. But if that were true, then Kate was probably telling the truth when she said that Ellis invited herself to The Hall that night. No, he thought, not necessarily. Kate could have invited Ellis and it was just unfortunate that Ellis marked it down in her diary. Having found that out, Kate came up with the Dawling idea to throw them off the scent. She knew that it was something that Ellis talked about.

Owen had already pointed all of this out to Ross and now Ross had to admit it made sense. He simply wished that it was a hypothesis that he felt more comfortable with. Perhaps he ought to ask himself why it was that he was being so stubborn. The woman was probably guilty and playing him for a fool, which was clearly what Owen thought.

"All right," Ross said, "just answer me two things. I'll give you motive if you give me timing. Why kill

Ellis Martin on February fourth? She broke with
Grainger nearly a year ago. So why now?" Owen
leaned back and spread his hands out.

"I don't know yet," he said. "But I will. A new
argument? Fresh motivation of some kind? Maybe
just a long festering of an old wound. I don't know,
but I'll find out."

"And the earring?" asked Ross.

"The easy explanation is that it's Kate's. It's real all
right, and the setting is new. Not remarkable, but not
shoddy. It could have come from any one of virtually
a hundred jewelry stores in the city, one or two in
Tunbridge Wells. We're checking with photos of Kate,
Ellis, David, and DeWarre to see if anyone can
identify them. It's a very long shot, to put it mildly. I
have also contacted the insurance companies for all
four of them to see if anything matching that description is insured. If we find that DeWarre either purchased or insured them, well, I don't know what the
hell that means."

"Highly unlikely," said Ross, "but worth checking.
You did check with Mary Jepp?"

"Since she's the only woman known to have visited
the site, I did. She said it was a very nice earring and
that she'd never seen it before. There is a chance that
it's a red herring, nothing to do with this at all."

"A McGuffin?" asked Ross, smiling.

"What's that when it's at home?" asked Owen.

"Ask William DeWarre," said Ross.

Owen had clearly decided to let this pass as further
evidence that Ross was, as Kendal would have said,
"going wonky." Instead he said, "Speaking of
DeWarre, he's going to be a wealthy fella."

"Oh," said Ross, "the will?"

"That's right. We heard this afternoon, just after you dragged me off to talk to that demented lorry owner. It's DeWarre, lock, stock, and barrel. Hardly a surprise."

"No," said Ross, "I suppose not. You didn't, by any chance, find out when she made it?"

"I did," said Owen. "She made it just about four months ago, after they got engaged. Prior to that she had had another will standing. The recipient was David Grainger. For everything." Ross looked at him.

"I'm not surprised by that either," he said.

"No," said Owen. "I just wonder if Grainger knew that it had been changed?"

"He must have assumed?"

"One would think so," said Owen, "but you never know."

"All right," said Ross, "get on with it. Find out about the state of Kate Davidson's scarf collection and I want someone, preferably two people, to place Ellis Martin, with or without one of them, either in that wood or somewhere else after twelve noon on the fourth. And Owen—" Ross caught him just as he was going out of the doorway. "Just do one more thing for me, will you?"

"Your wish is my command, Master," Owen said. That, thought Ross, was the reward for letting him have his own way.

"Get me some information on Dawling," said Ross. "I'm interested in his bank accounts. Do it quietly, mind."

"What am I looking for?" asked Owen. "The usual?"

"Or the unusual, yes," said Ross. "You know the stuff: anything sizable, irregular, or generally suspect, the stuff that frauds are made of."

"Will do," said Owen. "Oh, and by the way, we've not been able to find that wretched temp from Canterbury yet. Apparently she's gone on holiday with a friend somewhere. You know, pissing off, no word about when she's likely to return. Railcards and the open road type thing. We've spoken to her parents and they'll let us know as soon as she surfaces. I shouldn't think that it will turn out to matter all that much," he added. "We can be pretty certain that that call was made by either Grainger or Davidson."

Ross remained silent.

He sat in his office staring out of the window for some ten minutes after Owen had left. A sense of heaviness had come over him and it seemed momentarily impossible that he would ever have the energy to get up from this uncomfortable chair again. This case had been going on for less than a week and yet he felt as if he had been dealing with the ins and outs of Ellis Martin for years. What, he asked himself for the thousandth time, had the stupid girl done to get herself whacked on the head with a spade? Was it really because she had stolen her friend's lover and then treated him quite as badly as she had? She had treated him rather horribly, Ross thought. But then, there were two sides to every story. They would never hear Ellis Martin's. Was it really possible that Kate Davidson or David Grainger, or both of them, had considered what she had done worth killing for?

It was certainly possible, Owen had him there. Perhaps Grainger didn't know about the will. Perhaps it was money and that was why it had happened now.

Perhaps Grainger had thought that he'd better get on with it before she changed the will, not realizing that he was months too late. Ross could hardly believe that. Kate obviously had money of her own and Grainger didn't look as if he was on his way to the workhouse. So, if they had done it, why had they done it now? People don't just up and kill someone, Ross said to himself. There had to be a reason for why they had chosen to do it when they did. That was the only thing that Owen's theory refused to account for, the timing. The timing, thought Ross, and Billy Carter's treasure.

He reached into his drawer and brought out the little white cardboard box. The earring sat on its piece of tissue paper.

"I do not believe in coincidence," Ross said out loud. And then he reached for the telephone.

Kate Davidson answered on the second ring. Ross wondered if she'd been waiting for a call, and if so, from whom? Certainly not me, he thought. Her voice was slightly breathless and she sounded rather deflated when he announced himself, although she was far too polite to actually say, "Oh, it's you."

Instead she said, "Hello, Chief Inspector, how can I help you?" And Ross, after apologizing, proceeded to tell her.

The solicitor's firm of Craig, Holden, and White had offices in Gray's Inn. The fine weather had finally given way to rain and although it was still warm, Theobald's Road looked drab and rather dirty. From the office window Ross watched the traffic creep by and thought that he couldn't remember it being so bad when he and Kendal had lived in town. Various reports stated that it got worse every year and he envisioned a London of the future that was nothing but a huge snarl of taxis and buses and young men in Vauxhall Astras talking on car phones. He told himself sharply that he was getting old and pessimistic and turned his mind back to the business at hand.

Very shortly the business at hand, in the form of Thomas Holden, solicitor for the Davidson family, appeared apologizing profusely for keeping Ross waiting.

"You do understand, Chief Inspector," said Thomas Holden as he settled himself behind his desk, "that under ordinary circumstances I should not be able to reveal anything at all to you of my dealings with the Davidson family. They have been clients of ours for some twenty years," he added. "However, after Miss Davidson's telephone call to me yesterday, I am only too glad to do anything that I can to help. I am not, however, certain that I can tell you anything of value."

"I'm grateful to you for taking the time," said Ross.

Mr. Holden pulled a file across the desk. "I understand that you are interested in some work we did for the Davidsons last year on a planning application for, let me see, what was it?"

"A haulage depot," said Ross.

"That's right," said Mr. Holden. "The haulage depot that was being built adjoining The Hall. An awful thing."

"You acted for them in trying to bring about a judicial review of the planning procedure?"

Mr. Holden nodded. "That's right," he said.

"Could you tell me about it?" asked Ross. "About the grounds that you had for the case?"

"Well, that was it, really." Holden leaned back and tapped the arms of his chair in rhythm as he spoke. "It was one of those things where any logical human being could smell a rat. The area was designated for agricultural use. The parish council and the road safety authorities had advised against it and there was overwhelming public support for the refusal of permission."

"And yet permission was granted?"

"That's right," said Holden. "Permission was granted. That in itself was somewhat irregular."

"Irregular enough to constitute a case for review?" asked Ross.

"Unfortunately not. The council were, legally speaking, within their rights. You see, Chief Inspector, they have a great deal more power than you or I realize. They do not, for instance, have to follow government guidelines for designated use of land. Nor are they in any way liable under the law, either personally or as a body, unless you can find evidence of wrongdoing."

"Wrongdoing as in taking bribes, giving into undue influence, vested interest, that sort of thing?" Ross asked.

"I'm afraid so," said Holden. "It has to be that black and white."

"And in this case you couldn't find anything?" Holden shook his head.

"We did call in a barrister who agreed with us that, on the surface, it looked as though there had to be something that was not quite right about it. The decision appeared to be illogical to the point of suspicious."

"But you never found anything?" asked Ross.

"No, I'm afraid we didn't. And we did have a very good look."

"Did your enquiries concern a man called Dawling?"

"The fellow who owns the new depot?"

"That's right."

"They most certainly did," said Holden. "Quite naturally we looked into the background and the ownership of the company. It was quite reasonable, you see, that an irregularity there would have provided grounds for review."

"And you found nothing?"

"No, I'm afraid not."

"And you also looked into the dealings of the council?"

"Oh yes," said Holden, "very carefully. As I said before, you could smell a rat, but in this case, I'm afraid it's name was simply 'ambition.' I happened to know Aury Blaire and the way things were going it was obvious that he wasn't long for this world. Laura Ramsay is, I gather, an intelligent woman and the present government, like the old one, is frightfully keen on progress. Mrs. Ramsay, I gather, wants to be an MP and in order to get the nomination and party backing, she needed a feather in her cap."

"And along it came in the unlikely form of Dawling Haulage?" Holden smiled.

"Ambition makes strange bedfellows, doesn't it, Inspector? But I'm afraid it's as simple as that. It would have been just as useful to Laura Ramsay at the next General Election when she went up to oppose Blaire for the party backing. It simply turned out that she didn't have to wait that long. In a way," he added, "one would almost prefer something sinister. Naked ambition is rather embarrassing and it's so very banal."

Ross agreed. "People want to believe that they've been betrayed for grand reasons and, of course, most of the time it's all really quite ordinary. That, of course, adds insult to injury."

The rain grew heavier toward evening but it was still warm and balmy, more like spring than winter. What the Irish would call "soft weather," Ross thought, as he closed the doors of his garage and walked across the garden toward his house. He had bought it after Kendal died, when he had thrown over his career at New Scotland Yard and moved out into the countryside in some kind of effort to continue living. He might have felt that it was a betrayal of Kendal except that he knew that it was what she wanted him to do. She had said so during the last horrible weeks when he had all but lived in the hospital with her, when he had watched the woman he had known and loved vanish slowly in a fractured pastiche of tubes and machines until one day Kendal was indeed no longer there. All that remained to be done was to wheel the apparatus away and make arrangements for the funeral.

Despite the months of knowing that it would come, Ross had never quite been able to get used to it, would never be able to get used to it. He would never get used to the endless days of walking into offices or shops or the homes of friends with the words that were never meant for him running like a sick refrain through his mind, "my wife is dead."

It was a moment before Ross realized that he was

standing on the gravel path in the rain looking at the house. It had been nearly three years since Kendal died and this still happened, this weird time travel back to her that could hit him at the most unlikely moments. He supposed that it had come on just now because of his trip to London this afternoon. The rain was soaking through his gloves and making them slimy against the handle of his briefcase. He gave himself a small mental shake and, taking his keys out, opened the front door and let himself in.

Ross poured himself a generous whiskey and soda and looked at the sitting room, allowing a small measure of contentment to creep over him. He had had a bath and changed and lit the fire. Outside the rain continued, but here the curtains were pulled against it and the lamps were lit and Schubert was issuing forth from the stereo. The Queen Anne house was generously proportioned, beautiful both from the inside and the outside. At night, if the wind was from the right direction, you could just hear the sound of the sea from across the North downs. Of course, it was far too big for him and he hardly needed the fifteen acres of land that surrounded it. But the legacy of Kendal's money was not something that he allowed himself to feel guilty about. This house was something that they would have done together. Life, or rather death, thought Ross, had dictated that he should do it without her. But her absence made her no less a part of it. Despite the fact that she had never been here, Ross often felt her presence and that, more than anything, made it home.

He had left his slightly sodden briefcase in the front hall and now he fetched it and brought it into the sitting room. He settled into his favorite armchair and, pulling out a thick manila envelope, started to read the report that Henry Matchum had begun for Ellis Martin.

It was titled simply "Clara Beale" and the story was not a happy one. Clara was the fourth of six children of Louise and William Beale of Cairndale, a mining village in Wales. She was born in 1950 with brain damage. Clara lived at home for the first fifteen years of her life. In 1965 her father died of emphysema and Clara's mother was put on a state assistance program. Two of the younger children were sent to foster homes and Clara was sent to a "special school" in Cardiff.

By all accounts Clara was a placid child who grew into a placid adolescent with the mental age of approximately four years old. She spent five unremarkable years at Cardiff, during which time her mother died, also of emphysema. In 1970, when Clara Beale was twenty years old, the Cardiff school shut down and Clara was moved to a hospital for the mentally unstable. It was the five-hundred-bed establishment in Yorkshire called Briarcliffe.

Once installed at Briarcliffe, Clara's behavior began to deteriorate. She became temperamental, requiring special attention and frequent disciplinary action. By 1972 she was moved into a ward for "disturbed women." Clara developed a reputation for tantrums and it became increasingly difficult to deal with her. The ward was chronically understaffed with forty patients cared for by three orderlies and two nurses and placed under the overall management of a floor supervisor.

Given the state of affairs, it was only a matter of time before accidents began to happen. In the early hours of the morning of May 15, 1972, Clara Beale apparently went into an uncontrollable temper tantrum. She escaped from a nurse, ran down a flight of back stairs and fell over a banister and into the stairwell below. She died on impact. She was twenty-two years old.

Clara Beale's death was subject to a routine inter-hospital enquiry. It was established that she died in an unfortunate accident and the coroner signed a death certificate to that effect. The body was hastily cremated and no one thought further of the episode. No one, that was, except Tommy Haines, who had been an orderly on Clara's ward. He had been keeping an eye on her for some time. His intentions, he admitted, might not have been entirely honorable, but all the same, Tommy had something of a conscience and by mid-June it was bothering him mightily. Tommy lived at home with his sister Karen, a bright lass. After listening to what Tommy had to tell her, she marched him straight off to the police.

Shortly thereafter, Clara Beale had her hour in the spotlight. Unfortunately, she wasn't around to appreciate it. On close examination it was revealed that the last two years of Clara Beale's short life had been a living hell. Between 1970 and 1971 she had been the victim of a number of mysterious "accidents" that required no less than twenty visits to the hospital infirmary, some of them prolonged. In the first four and a half months of 1972, there had been eleven such visits. Under police pressure, infirmary doctors and floor orderlies began to remember more about Clara Beale. What they remembered involved a catalog of broken bones, abrasions, cuts, bruises, and burns, some of the latter suspiciously resembling those made by cigarette ends.

The records that could have backed up the allega-
tions had mysteriously disappeared. There was no
body to autopsy, thanks to the hospital's policy of
swift cremation. But there were stories and many of
them featured patients other than Clara Beale, patients still at Briarcliffe. A large majority of them just
happened to be in the same ward that Clara Beale had
been in.

The newspapers ate the story alive. There were
questions in The House. The BBC made a documentary. And, finally, Briarcliffe's doors were permanent-
ly closed.

At the end of the report Harry Matchum had added
a few further notes: "As Miss Martin requested,
traced members of Clara B.'s family. Brother Edward,
now 45, emigrated to Canada, 1969. Sister Amanda
seen in London, 1978. Married, divorced, believed to
have changed name. Am guessing she is now in her
forties. (Cairndale records in county office which was
partially destroyed by fire in 1961.) No idea about
other brother, who is, I think, the oldest, or about two
children, boy and girl, who were put into care. Am
guessing they would now be in their late twenties,
early thirties. I can pursue this if you like. The nurses,
two supervisors, and several orderlies and doctors
were sacked. There was some talk of criminal pro-
ceedings but case was dropped due to 'lack of evidence.' Hoped this helped, all the best—Harry
Matchum."

With the package, Harry had included one eight by
ten photograph. On the back he had simply printed,
"Clara Beale." Ross turned it over and looked into the
lovely, vacant face. She was blond with large eyes and
delicate features. There was an innocence about her,

an eternal childishness. In the photo she was smiling. Harry had noted that it was her "graduation" picture from Cardiff. So, Ross thought sadly, she had still smiled then.

Looking at the photo, he could understand Tommy Haines's desire for this girl. Perhaps it was not purely lascivious after all. Perhaps something in him wanted to protect her. Had Ellis felt the same thing? Had Ellis Martin seen this lovely, empty face and felt horror and shock at what had been done to it? Was that why she wanted to know about Clara Beale? Could that be why she had contacted Matchum, paid him handsomely, gone to all that trouble? Matchum had told Ross that Ellis wanted to know about Clara Beale's family. Ross sat with the picture of Clara Beale on his lap and wondered.

Chapter
15
·

It was 1:00 A.M. before Ross finally turned out the lights and went to bed. He slept badly and woke early.

Harry Matchum had given Ross his home number and, all things considered, Ross thought he excercised admirable restraint in waiting until seven-thirty to dial it. Something told him Mr. Matchum was an early riser and apparently he was right. Having assured Ross that he'd already been out and run what he referred to as "the bloody five miles," Matchum said, "So, Chief Inspector, you got my little bundle of joy, did you? I didn't have time to do much on it. Sorry for that."

"Not at all," said Ross. "It's been most helpful, Mr. Matchum."

"Mr. Matchum's my old dad," he said, laughing. "You'd better call me Harry or I won't know who you're talking about. What can I do for you, Inspector?"

"I'm interested in your notes on the Beale family," said Ross. "Can you tell me, was that something that Ellis Martin was particularly interested in?"

"The Beales?" asked Harry. "You could say so. Wanted to look at all the principals, as she called them. Family, staff, administrators, the lot. She wanted pictures in particular, anything I could dig up. So far I'd only found that one of our Clara, as far as the family went. Funnily enough some more I was chasing arrived yesterday after I'd given that stuff to your chap. Send them on to you, shall I?"

"If you would," said Ross.

"Shame about the Beale family," Matchum continued. "Of course I didn't have the kind of time to work on it I would have liked and it makes it tricky when they all split up like that. County records office burning to the ground doesn't help, mind."

"No," said Ross, "I don't suppose it does. Ellis Martin didn't indicate why it was she was so interested in the case and in the Beale family, did she?"

"Not beyond the old film routine," he replied, "which I'm not sure I believed in the first place. I mean if that was the case why would she care about what became of them all? I don't know, maybe she was going to do a follow-up project, you know, 'The Legacy of Clara Beale, How Briarcliffe Affected Their Lives.' I'm damned if I know, Inspector. I never actually met her. She was just a voice on the phone to me. She paid me well and she wanted to know what's become of them. All I can tell you."

"I see," said Ross.

"You reckon there's more to it than that, do you, Chief Inspector?" asked Matchum.

"I really don't know," Ross said.

Kate put her feet up on the edge of her desk and flipped the tab on a beer can as she listened to the telephone ringing in her brother's office six thousand miles away in San Francisco. She still found it hard to believe that she could dial a number and talk to Rob somewhere on the other side of the world. Now, as she heard his familiar voice, she wondered if, at last, she was going to cry.

"Hey there, what's up?" Rob asked. At age thirty-five he still talked like a frat brother from Sigma Nu. Kate assumed it was because he'd gone to Berkeley and never quite recovered. She wondered if that was what all that sunshine did to your brain.

"Nothing much is 'up,'" Kate replied, "except for the fact that the local police seem to believe that I've murdered Ellis."

"Oh Kates," Rob said, "have they got anything yet? Do they still think it was David?"

"I'm not joking," Kate said, taking a sip of beer. "They honestly are inclined to think it was me, or the two of us in it together."

Rob laughed. "You and David knocking Ellis off and dumping her in the woods?"

"That's right," said Kate. "And it's not funny."

"No, you're right," he said, "it isn't. Have you talked to Holden?"

"Briefly," she said. "I'm to say nothing until he gets here if they actually bring me in for questioning, which so far they haven't. That would be the final irony, wouldn't it? If I end up doing life for murdering

Ellis without having actually got the satisfaction of doing it?"

"What amazes me about all this is that someone didn't kill Ellis a long time ago. Do you remember that Sunday about twenty years ago when Dad took us all to the Easter point to point? I would say that Ellis has been a candidate for violent death in my book since about then."

Kate did remember. She and Ellis had been no more than eight or nine and had then been best friends. Rob and David must have been twelve or so and Ellis spent a lot of time dragging around behind them and giggling. That particular day Rob had nearly murdered her when she had lost the winning tickets for a horse that had come in on impossibly long odds. The five pounds that Kate's father had put up for a stake was gone, along with some substantial winnings. In Rob's eyes, Ellis had been earmarked for bodily harm from that day forward.

They chatted for a few more minutes. Kate asked after her sister-in-law and after the state of Rob's business. He was an architect who specialized in beautiful houses for beautiful people. After saying that he hoped she'd come to California soon, if she wasn't in jail, they hung up.

The conversation didn't leave Kate feeling greatly cheered. Suddenly The Hall seemed like a very big house, cavernous and empty. She wandered into the kitchen for a cup of tea. She had spent the morning trying to work on a set design that she was doing for a new production coming up in the West End. As a rule, she didn't like theater work and tried to avoid it, but this was a project that had excited her. Now, however, she couldn't muster much of an interest in anything.

Earlier in the day she'd spent several hours in her studio staring at blank pieces of paper and doodling on the edge of the script. Being suspected of murder was, she decided, distinctly unpleasant.

Rob had been trying to be helpful by being funny, but the truth was far from humorous. Ellis was dead and she and David were suspects. David had come up for a drink last night and they had done their best to avoid the subject, but that was as unsuccessful as talking about it had been. They had even pretended they were in love again, but that hadn't worked out very well, either. Ellis, alive or dead, had truly put the kibosh on that, Kate thought. Just like Ellis. She wasn't terribly different at all, now that she was dead.

Kate filled the kettle and switched it on. She remembered the day Rob mentioned as though it were yesterday, which was unusual since she had a reputation for not being able to remember her name from one moment to the next. But the sense of outrage and injustice that filled that long-ago Easter was quite clear in her mind, just slightly dulled by the passage of some twenty-odd years. Ellis had been holding their tickets from the tout. David had chosen a horse that was running at ten-to-one odds. Kate could even remember its name, Foreign Affair. Kate and Rob had put their five pound notes on it to win, following David's example. Ellis hadn't fancied the name or the risk and had put her fiver on the favorite. When Foreign Affair came home well ahead of the field, the favorite comfortably well back, they thought that the world had come to a halt. They would have had fifty pounds each, an awful lot at ages nine and twelve. Ellis, of course, had come up empty. And then she had lost the tickets. Or claimed to have done.

Bitterness had soaked the rest of the day. Ellis had made it worse by crying when they had refused to speak to her. In the car on the way home Ellis sat in the front with Kate's father while the others rode in back. Kate remembered that they had halfheartedly played the license plate game, refusing to allow Ellis to join in. But they couldn't even get up much enthusiasm for that.

Kate very nearly dropped the mug that she was holding. For a moment she could barely move and when she did put the mug down, her hands were trembling. She started to go to the telephone and then she stopped. Instead she walked straight out of the kitchen door. As she disappeared around the edge of the garages, the kettle boiled, whistled and turned itself off.

Ross noticed the red Porsche as soon as he turned into the station drive. It was parked at a distinctly rakish angle, almost directly under his office window. He wondered if she was there of her own free will or because Owen had summoned her. Constable Glen, on desk duty, answered the question for him almost as soon as he walked through the door.

"Miss Davidson's waiting in your office, sir," he said. "She says it's very important."

Kate was standing by the window. She must have watched him arrive. She spun around almost before he got through the door and he could see that she was very excited.

"I've remembered!" she exclaimed. He closed the door and looked at her. "I've remembered about Tinker Wood," she said. "About the day I was walking there. I'm almost certain that it was that Friday. I knew that there was something familiar about it, I knew it. And then Rob reminded me about the license plate game and I remembered. Oh Christ," she said, laughing, "I am such an idiot! I can't remember a thing from one second to the next. You know, my father always told me it would get me in trouble and it bloody nearly did!"

"Calm down," said Ross. "Now, go very, very slowly."

"Great Big Harry," Kate announced and something close to a look of triumph spread across her face. Then she began to laugh again. "Oh, Inspector," she said, "I'm so sorry. You must think I've gone mad. You see, when you asked me if I'd seen anything in Tinker Wood that day, well, something kept hovering at the back of my mind, something that I couldn't quite get a hold of."

"Go on," said Ross.

"Well, now I know what it was, and why it stuck in my mind. You see, when we were children we used to watch police programs on TV and you know how they're always calling out license plate numbers with that alphabet? You know," she waved her hands impatiently, "Delta, Charlie, Tango, 2, 3, 4?"

"Ah, yes," said Ross.

"Right," she said. "Well, when we were children we could never remember the proper alphabet call words, so we made up our own. We used to call out license plates of cars that passed us while we were driving. It sent my parents around the twist."

"I can imagine."

"Quite. Well, you see, my father had this Jaguar and the letters on its registration were GBH. So we used to call it Great Big Harry." She paused, waiting for Ross to understand what it was that she was trying to tell him. Sadly, he remained in the dark.

"Go on," he said.

"When I was in Tinker Wood, just after I had turned off the footpath—"

"The one that runs below the old drive and the cottage?"

"That's right. I stopped because my boot lace had snapped. And as I was trying to knot it, I looked back toward the lane. I suppose it must have been the noise that made me look up, and I did see a car. It stopped at the end of the lane and it indicated and it stuck in my head, I guess. The picture of it stopped there stuck because its license letters were GBH, Great Big Harry."

Ross sat down in his chair and stared at her.

"What kind of car?"

"Oh God, I wouldn't know." She shook her head. "But it was white. Kind of old-fashioned looking, nothing fancy. It had an ordinary boot, you know, not a hatchback. I only glanced up."

"Can you remember anything else about it?" he asked.

"No," she said, sitting down. "I'm sorry. All I have in my mind is this mental picture of the car stopped there with its indicator light blinking and those letters on the license plate. I was still bent over, fiddling with my boot, and I just glanced up and there it was like that and then it drove off."

"Which indicator light?"

"The left. It turned left into the May Green road."

"The driver?" She shook her head.

"No. It was some ways away and I was behind it."

"Did they see you?" Ross asked.

"I don't think so," she said. "I was more or less looking through the bushes."

"And you're certain that it was Friday the fourth, the day you walked to The Snipe for lunch?"

"No," she said, "I am not absolutely certain that that was the day that I saw the car, but I think that it was. I think so because I haven't been up there since and because the boot lace had snapped. I haven't changed it and I would have changed it if I'd gone walking again. But I haven't been walking since the fourth."

She leaned back in her chair and closed her eyes. Ross noticed that she looked tired again and he felt sympathy for her. She was too intelligent not to understand what Owen suspected her of.

"Would you like a cup of coffee, Miss Davidson?" he asked. "It's not very nice, but it's usually hot." She opened her eyes and looked at him for a moment and then she stood up.

"No thanks, Inspector," she said, smiling. "As a matter of fact, I think I left the kettle boiling."

Chapter
16

It could be nothing," said Owen. "It could be someone who'd just been at the pub. It doesn't match any
of the vehicle descriptions from the lunchtime drink-
ers," he added, "but that could be an oversight on our
part." Ross could tell by the tone of Owen's voice that
he was trying to prepare himself for disappointment.
Still, the excitement seeped through. The lane came to
a dead end at The Snipe. If the car in question hadn't
been from the pub, it must have been from one of the
six cottages that lined the lane. There were, of course,
other alternatives. Someone having a picnic, someone
who was lost, someone turning around. Or someone
who had just met Ellis Martin.

"It could be nothing," Owen repeated.

"It could be," Ross agreed. "That's what we're
going to find out."

Ross drove up the lane beside Tinker Wood and
stopped in front of one of the cottages. It was small
and very neat. The white paint job and green trim had

been recently touched up. Dierdre Carter was in the garden hanging clothes on the washing line. A little girl was standing beside her holding an enamel basin filled with clothespins.

"Good afternoon, Mrs. Carter," Ross said, as he got out of the car. "I'm Inspector Ross and this is Inspector Davies." The little girl smiled at them and sidled around behind her mother. Dierdre held the bundle of laundry in both hands and watched them come across the garden toward her.

Ross felt rather badly at having surprised her this way, but he had hardly had a choice. The Carters did not have a telephone. Now Dierdre Carter looked at him and said, "Has Billy done something?" Her voice trailed off into a thin whisper of fear.

"No, no," Ross said quickly. "Nothing's wrong, Mrs. Carter. Billy's been a great help and you should be proud of him." This appeared to relax her slightly and Ross went on. "In fact," he said, "I was hoping that Billy could help us with one more thing. Is he here at the moment?"

Dierdre nodded and, turning to the little girl, said, "Lin, go and fetch your brother." Linda put the bowl down on the grass and ran away to the back of the cottage.

"Will you come in?" Dierdre asked, clearly hoping they wouldn't.

Ross shook his head. "It's very kind of you, Mrs. Carter," he said, "but we're in a bit of a hurry and we won't bother you."

At that moment Billy appeared around the edge of the house with his sister behind him. He looked at Ross and Owen and dug his hands into his pockets as he came toward them.

"Hello, Billy," said Ross. "How are you?" Billy nodded, watching his mother. "I wanted to ask you something, Billy," said Ross. "I need your help." Billy looked at Ross with a flicker of interest and nodded mutely.

"Answer the Inspector, Billy," said his mother.

"All right," Billy whispered.

"I want you to try to remember," Ross said. "Were you playing in Tinker Wood on Friday the fourth of February? The day before you found the earring?"

Billy looked at Ross for a moment and then he said, "Fridays we get out of school early. In time to come home for dinner."

"Billy's supposed to help around here on Friday afternoons," his mother said, "but you're always running off, aren't you?"

Ross decided to let this pass and concentrated on Billy. So that was why the child was so reluctant to talk about Friday. He either had to admit to playing truant or lie to Ross.

"Billy," he said gently, "you did play in the wood that day, didn't you, on Friday, February fourth, the week before they found the lady?" Billy nodded.

"Yes," he said.

"Good," said Ross. "I'm very glad about that, because I need your help. Did you see anything, anything at all, while you were in the wood that day?" Ross held his breath while Billy considered his answer.

"Yes," Billy said.

"And what did you see, Billy?" Ross asked. Billy looked at his shoes for a moment and then he looked up at Ross.

"I saw a car," he said.

Ross felt a twinge of excitement pass through him and travel to Owen, whom he willed to be quiet.

"What kind of car?" Ross asked.

"It was a Rover," Billy said, "like Mr. Binn's got, but it was white."

"The Binns own the shop in May Green," Dierdre Carter said. "The one's got the post office in it."

"Did you see anything else, Billy?" Ross asked. "Anything at all?" Billy shook his head and looked at Ross.

"The car was in the old drive," he said. "It was parked there. I saw it from my secret place, where I showed you. But I had to come back here and help my Mum. I didn't see nothing else."

"Can you remember, do you have any idea when this was on Friday afternoon?" Ross asked.

"Right after I got home from school," Billy said, "before I had my dinner. I had to come back here for my dinner."

"That would have been at about two, Inspector," Dierdre Carter said. "The bus lets them off about one, but what with my work and collecting Lin and walking up here and all, I don't get home to get them their dinner until just before two."

"You've both been a great help," he said.

"Billy," Owen could no longer contain himself, "why didn't you tell us this before?"

Billy looked from Owen to his mother to Ross and then he said, "You asked me about when I found the earring. Didn't ask me about the day before."

After leaving the Carters' cottage, Owen and Ross sat in the car for a moment.

"God preserve me from ever being at the mercy of the mind of an eight-year-old," said Owen.

185

Ross, who was staring at the windscreen as though it might contain the secrets of the universe, smiled.

"It's our own fault," he said, "but I second the sentiment." He turned the ignition. "For Christ's sake, make bloody certain that you take that child to see the Binns' car and be absolutely sure that we're all talking about the same make."

Ross pulled out into the narrow lane and started back toward Millbrook.

"Check everyone along any of these roads who might have seen the car at around 2:00 P.M. Farmers, gardeners, milkmen, village idiots, the lot. When you've identified the make of the car, circulate a bulletin, both local and nationwide. And then go through Wildesham and May Green with a fine-tooth comb."

"Starting with The Hall and the Grainger farm?"

"God, yes," said Ross. "Let's, for heaven's sake, get that out of the way first. And then the Dawling garage—"

"You've got a bit of a thing about him, don't you, Master?"

Ross laughed. The mood of the day had changed. "Yes, I suppose I do. It must be his endearing manner."

"I suppose that this puts Kate Davidson and David Grainger out of it? Given the fact that she identified the car."

"It certainly opens it up, doesn't it?" replied Ross.

"Well," Owen said, "let's just hope that it doesn't open it up too much. Are you still hellbent on the planning conspiracy theory?"

"I don't know," said Ross, as they pulled into the

station drive. "At the moment we still haven't a lot of anything to go on."

"No," said Owen. "And it will be a lovely day when we find this damned car and it turns out to belong to a traveling salesman who was having a pee after one too many in The Snipe."

Ross pulled up in front of the station and stopped.

"Not coming in?" Owen asked.

Ross shook his head. "One more wild goose to chase," he said. "Let me know as soon as you have anything." Owen waved at him and disappeared through the station doors.

Ross had been meaning to make this call for some time and when he thought about it later he couldn't understand why he hadn't got around to it. He supposed that, in his mind, the man was a suspect and that he had been wary of treading on Owen's toes. Still, he thought, here was the one person who ought to know Ellis Martin better than anyone. He had been her childhood friend, her lover, and her fiancé. Surely if there was some clue to Ellis Martin's past that would lead Ross to those final moments on the afternoon of February fourth, David Grainger would have some idea of what it might be.

David was in one of the large dutch barns stacking bales. He saw Ross drive in and waved to him from the top of the stack before he climbed down the ladder and met him in the yard.

"Inspector," he called, "how are you?" Ross knew that he would have talked to Kate, would have heard about the car and would have realized that the police now had something more interesting than his possible homicidal tendencies to speculate on. The relief on his face was evident. Ross found himself hoping that it wouldn't be unjustified.

He was wearing wellingtons and an old barbour over a fisherman's sweater. Despite his size and dark coloring there was something gentle about him, a shyness. He and Ellis would have looked nice together, thought Ross. Her petite figure and blond hair would have been set off against his size. Both of them had blue eyes. Shaking David's hand and following him into the house, Ross wondered at this man's personal acquaintance with pain.

It was a house that ought to have children in it, Ross thought, as they made their way toward the kitchen. It was big and sunlit and its wide oak floors and bright rooms called out for the chaos of a family. There was about it an aura of waiting, of being held in suspended time. It was the home of a single man. Probably a lonely man, perhaps one who moved through this house watching the approach of his mid-thirties and wondering how long it was before it was too late.

"Have some tea," said David, pushing a chair out from the kitchen table. "I don't, as a rule, but I always forget how much I like it. There may even be a biscuit here. My housekeeper is convinced that I'll starve to death unless supplied with an endless stream of biscuits." Ross watched him as he put the kettle on the Aga and measured three teaspoons of tea carefully into the pot.

"Did you always want to be a farmer?" he asked.

"Yes," said David, "at least on this farm. My family has lived here for generations."

He took two teacups and saucers out of the cupboard and set them on the table. No electric kettle and no mugs here. The tea service was Royal Worcester, probably David's grandmother's. No, Ross thought, this wasn't the sort of thing that Ellis Martin would have understood.

Instead of quality, history, a caring for places and things, she would have seen a trap, a dead end as a well-to-do provincial farmer's wife. She would not have had the interior resources of someone like Kate to get her through the long winter afternoons and evenings. The stability that houses and families like this represented would have seemed a cage to Ellis. She wanted safety, thought Ross, but she was a yearner, a restless rearranger who could never concentrate her energy for quite long enough to find solace or even self-expression. Then he realized that that was what was missing. In everything of Ellis's that he had come into contact with there had been quality, obvious care, a sense of meticulousness and even beauty. But there had been no imagination, no sense of personal expression. She was lost, thought Ross. From place to place and man to man and project to project, landscape gardening to documentaries, she was looking for somewhere to belong. For a while, perhaps she thought she could find it in this house. If she had waited long enough, perhaps she would have found it, Ross thought, and she might be alive today.

David poured the tea. He set a cup in front of Ross and asked, "Did you always want to be a policeman?"

Ross smiled and reached for the sugar. "No," he said, "I wanted to be a famous composer and a great novelist and, at one time, a fighter pilot. I always envied people who knew just what they wanted to be."

"Most people consider it boring," David said, offering him a biscuit.

"Did Ellis?" David took a biscuit off the plate and looked at it before biting into it.

"Not at first," he said. "That came later, when reality reared its ugly head."

"The baby?" David nodded.

"Yes. That was when Ellis realized what it would really be like to live here and be married to me. That's something about farmers, Inspector. They don't have too much trouble dealing with reality on a day-to-day basis. You can't avoid it. If it rains you get wet, if you see what I mean."

"Yes," said Ross.

"Reality wasn't really Ellis's strong point," David said. "That was part of her considerable charm. She was shades of Peter Pan in a never-never world that most of us mortals can't dwell in for very long. For a start, most of us can't afford it, and even if we could, I don't think we'd find it very satisfying. Illusions are lovely, but Ellis wanted to live off spun sugar. Pretty, but not very nourishing in the long run." David stopped and smiled at him. "Unfortunately," he added, "babies are very real and so are husbands."

"How old was Ellis when her parents were killed?" asked Ross.

"Oh, I don't know, exactly," David said. "Tiny. Two. At most, three."

"Do you know anything about them?"

David thought for a moment and then shook his head. "No, actually," he said. "Now that I think about it, I don't think I ever actually heard them spoken about. They weren't from this area, I do know that. Ellis's father was Jane Martin's brother, I do know that. Ellis just belonged to her aunt and that was all we ever thought of it."

"I see," Ross said. "Did she talk about her parents at all, ask about them, wonder about them?"

"Not to me," said David. "I don't recall her ever expressing any interest in them whatsoever."

"That's odd, don't you think?" Ross asked.

"Possibly," said David. "Possibly not. She may have talked about it with her aunt and settled whatever questions she had."

"Tell me about something else," said Ross. "Tell me about this planning business, about Ellis's concern with it. That must have started before you—" He was trying to find the delicate phrase, but David finished the sentence for him.

"Before she left me? Yes, it had, just. And yes, Ellis was very worked up about it from the start."

"Was that uncharacteristic?"

"Not at all," said David, smiling. "You see, Ellis really did love this area, this village. Even Ellis had to have something concrete, Inspector, and this village and that house were really all that she had of her own. But there was more to it than that. I think it offended her sense of propriety, her idea of what an English village should be, if you see what I mean."

"They don't usually feature haulage depots?"

"No," said David. "And of course, she didn't much care for Dawling either. Though that can't take much explaining."

"Did she actually ever come into contact with him?" Ross asked.

"I shouldn't have thought so," David said, "but that would hardly have made a difference. Ellis was a frightful snob."

"The Kenneth Dawlings of this world didn't fit in with her idea of an English village either?"

"Most definitely not. Ellis thought that he was a common little upstart and the idea that he could do this thing to 'her village' quite enraged her. That's what I meant about her problem with reality, Inspector. In Ellis's version of country life there were lovely big houses run by gracious ladies and staffed by grateful and loyal retainers and the countryside was dotted with well-kept, prosperous farms run by happy farmers."

"I see," said Ross. "No channel tunnels and no haulage depots?" David smiled.

"No channel tunnels and very definitely no haulage depots," he said. "Mind you," he added, "Dawling is rather a pig, if you'll pardon the expression. He made himself thoroughly objectionable over the whole affair. First of all there was the business of not notifying local landowners and then, when everyone was protesting like Hell, he was strutting about like a bantam cock boasting that no matter what happened, he'd get his planning permission."

"This was before the parish council voted against it?"

"And afterward, which particularly enraged people, as you can imagine."

"After the parish council and the road commission advised against it, he was still going about saying he'd get planning permission?"

"That's right. As a matter of fact, I was in The Royal Oak the night after the parish council meeting. This particular night, Dawling came in. A couple of people were actually trying to be pleasant to him and said that they were sorry to hear about the parish council vote. Well, Dawling simply laughed in their faces and said that surely they couldn't think that that meant anything. Called them a bunch of village idiots, or something charming like that, and said that it was in the bag. The right people were backing him and anyone in the place could safely put money on the fact that he'd get permission for the depot."

"That's what he said?" Ross asked. David nodded and got up to refill the teapot.

"That's right. And it looks like he was right."

"Did anyone think anything of it at the time?" David put the teapot back on the table and sat down again.

"You mean suspect anything untoward?" He shook his head. "No. Dawling's an old windbag. That was the general consensus. I must admit that there were those who remembered it later, however."

"Ellis among them?"

"Apparently so, although we were not exactly friendly at the time. I gather that she went on a real campaign about Dawling. The rest of us knew how she could be when she got a hold of something, but from what I hear, Dawling wasn't all that amused—" He stopped suddenly and stared at Ross. "Oh, my God," he said quietly, "you're not suggesting?"

"I don't know," said Ross.

"Oh, dear me," said David slowly. "I honestly would find it hard to believe, Inspector. Dawling really is just a silly little man. But perhaps Ellis really did find something out about him?"

"There's no evidence of that," Ross said.

"The idea is utterly ridiculous," David said. "I can't imagine Dawling having the cash to bribe anyone for a start. Even if they'd take it, which I honestly can't see either. And surely he wouldn't go out and kill Ellis just because she annoyed him?"

"It's very difficult to say, but one wouldn't have thought so," said Ross.

David picked up another biscuit and broke it in half. "I must admit," he said, smiling, "I never thought I'd say it, but I can almost sympathize with Dawling at the moment. I'm waiting on planning permission for a new milking parlor and it's hell. I'm sure that if I could think of someone to bribe, I'd have a go."

"Well," said Ross, standing up, "you've been more than generous with your time, Mr. Grainger."

"David, please," he said, leading Ross down the passage toward the front door. "Come again when this is all over and have something stronger than tea."

"Thank you," Ross said, "I will."

They were walking across the yard toward Ross's car when David stopped and looked at him. "You're trying to tell me that we should have taken Ellis more seriously over all this, aren't you?" he asked. Ross considered the question and then shook his head.

"I'm not sure," he said, "we simply have to cover every possible angle."

"It just seems such nonsense," said David. Ross nodded in agreement.

It wasn't until later that he wondered whether David Grainger had been referring to the planning committee or to the killing of Ellis Martin. At that moment, Ross thought, he had to admit that personally he couldn't make much sense of either of them.

Chapter 17

Owen placed the tray on the edge of Ross's desk and looked at it with distaste. Ross had to admit that the donuts that adorned the pale green plate did not look particularly appetizing. Millbrook was not one of those picturesque little market towns filled to the brim with jolly bakers turning out mouth-watering concoctions by the dozen. At least they had managed to do something about the coffee. It now came from a machine that Owen had brought from home in a gesture of self-defense. He poured two cups and pushed the donut plate toward Ross.

"I suppose that those things are safe to eat?" Ross asked. He was not altogether certain from the feel of the one he had picked up, reminiscent of an old bath sponge. The sugar flaked off in a crust on the palm of his hand.

"Well?" Ross asked.

"I shouldn't think so," said Owen, sitting down. "Oh, I see, you mean the car." He grinned. "Well,

Master, it doesn't come from Wildesham or May Green or, so far, from the surrounding area. Not only are there no white four-door Rovers with the license 'GBH,' there are no white four-door Rovers at all. It seems that Rover stopped making that model some time ago. But, even if it's the new shape and not the old shape, and they are similar, we're out of luck."

Ross put the donut back on the plate and tried the coffee, a significant improvement.

"What about sightings?" Owen shook his head.

"No one can remember seeing it. But according to local lore in the shape of Constable Glen, that's not altogether unusual. Friday afternoon tends to be a pretty dead time. The school does close early, that's true. But on the whole, no one much is likely to be about, at least in May Green. The pub closes at three and the village shop, which is also the only shop, closes at twelve for the day. So, it is conceivable that at around the time that Kate Davidson says she saw the car leave, there weren't very many people about. The pub was pretty empty anyway and most people had gone by the time she left. The others were apparently there until well after three o'clock, as is local custom for regulars. Also, if the car did turn left, as our Miss Davidson thinks, then it would have turned toward the crossroads. It needn't have gone into May Green at all. It could well have gone straight across the crossroads and down into the lane that leads away from May Green and joins up with the main road to Wildesham about a mile later."

"And if someone didn't want to be seen, that's the route they'd take? Risking, of course, meeting someone head on in a narrow lane?"

"That's right," said Owen. "Of the two options, I

suspect that's the less risky, in the long run. There's only one small farm on that lane, whereas the other way you have to go right through May Green and, incidentally, come right into Wildesham at the crossroads. Or, if you turn the other way at the May Green crossroads you have to drive through a fair number of houses before you're clear on the other side."

"This rather changes things, doesn't it?" Ross said. "It may be that we're no longer looking for someone local at all. In which case we have two options. Someone who didn't know Ellis and somehow got a hold of her, killed her and dumped her in Tinker Wood, or—"

"Or the possibility of someone who did know Ellis but didn't come from here. Someone who either killed her up there or killed her elsewhere."

"How did they get a hold of the spade?" Ross asked.

"I don't know," said Owen. "Could it have been left at the edge of the wood, or even in the wood? From work being done on the Grainger farm some time ago?"

"Grainger says not," said Ross. "But that doesn't mean it's impossible. I do wish that someone had seen that bloody girl some time after noon on the fourth. This doesn't actually lead us anywhere helpful, does it?" he asked.

"It does put David Grainger and the Davidson girl out of it, at least a bit," said Owen. "Unless we can tie them to a white Rover. Unless, of course, the damn Rover doesn't have anything to do with anything. Incidentally," he added, smiling, "we did have a routine look around the Dawling garages."

"Oh, yes," said Ross, "and how did our Mr. Dawling like that?"

"Not very much," Owen said. "He liked it even less when we turned up at Casa Dawling. Where, incidentally, we found no trace of a white Rover. But there is one thing that I thought you might like to know. His wife has pierced ears."

"Along with two-thirds of the rest of the world's females," said Ross. He took a bite of the donut which indeed tasted of old bath sponge, then said, "All right, find the damn car. Start with garages and rental agencies within a twenty-mile radius and if that doesn't give you anything, open it out to fifty miles and so on. You've still got a national bulletin out?"

"That's right," Owen said, standing up, "and there is something else. We had a damn good nose around Dawling's bank statements and the state of his finances in general."

"And?" asked Ross, knowing full well what the answer would be.

"There's nothing out of the ordinary," said Owen. "Nothing at all. I can tell you that if he was bribing anybody he was pawning the family silver to do it. I'm afraid that, uncharming though he is, our local haulage magnate simply isn't in that league."

After Owen had gone, Ross sat for some time at his desk. He finished the unpalatable donut and poured himself another cup of coffee. He unscrewed his ink pen and drew a series of doodles along the side of his blotter. They were small furry sheep jumping over a procession of hurdles.

Ross felt he had but one course open to him and that would involve widening the net considerably, delving far back into Ellis Martin's past. The answers were not here in Kent. He would have to send a team up to Somerset House to the Public Records Office to see if they could find the records of Ellis Martin's adoption and birth. People would have to be traced and interviewed, whole new avenues of enquiry would have to be opened up. It would mean a considerable commitment of police hours and resources and even then it very well might turn up nothing. He would give Owen forty-eight hours to locate the car and then they would begin again.

There was a knock on the door. He shouted, "Come in," and a WPC entered and placed a brown envelope on his desk. It was Ellis Martin's mail that would have been delivered to the house in Wildesham, had she been there to receive it.

Ross opened the envelope and two bills fell out. One was from the Gas Board and one was from Access. Being dead didn't make your mail any more interesting. All the same, he opened the two bills and read them.

She owed the Gas Board £75.60 and they weren't happy about it. He put the gas bill aside and turned to the Access bill which covered the billing period from the previous month. A quick glance told him that there were no charges at all from Harvey Nichols. She had not bought one of Kate's scarves in the month before she died. She had bought quite a few other things, however. Miss Martin obviously did rather a lot of her conspicuous consuming in Harrods. She had also purchased tickets to a cinema in the West End and to a play, both of which were in her diary. Ross ran his eye down the column of purchases and was about to put the bill aside when something caught his eye. He looked at his desk calendar and then looked at the Access bill again. There it was, a charge from British Rail for £2.30 for a return ticket from Paddington to Colindale on January fifth. Unless he was very much mistaken, there was only one reason that Ross could think of for anyone wanting to go to Colindale.

It was a particularly drab part of North London. In the past, Ross had frequently gone to Colindale to lecture at the Metropolitan Police Training Center. Afterward, on occasion, he had cheered himself by indulging his childhood fantasies of the wild blue yonder, paying a quick visit to the RAF museum at Hendon. But neither of these attractions brought him to Colindale this afternoon. Nor had the enormous and inordinately depressing facade of the Colindale Hospital, which he was fairly certain that Ellis Martin would have had no reason to visit. Indeed, the only place in this unremittingly gray semi-urban spread that he could see having any attraction at all for Ellis Martin was that which attracted most visitors to Colindale: the newspaper archive housed in the Colindale library.

As every journalist, researcher, and most policemen know, Colindale Library houses the only newspaper archive in the London area. It is an exceptionally good one, carrying data on microfiche that goes back somewhere beyond the dawn of time. Now, as Ross parked and opened the front door of his car for Police Constable Marshall, he said a silent prayer that Ellis had come here for the obvious reason rather than to visit some obscure and destitute relative who was a deep dark secret and would remain forever as such, lost in this wilderness of council estates and semi-detached villas.

"Chief Inspector," said the Head Librarian, as she

welcomed them into her tiny office, "I hope we can be of help to you."

"So do I," said Ross, shaking her hand. "This is Constable Thomas Marshall, who will, I'm afraid, be doing the inevitable leg work. Unless, of course, we get lucky with someone's memory."

"Yes," said the Head Librarian, "I'm afraid that that's rather unlikely, given the huge number of people who do research here. But after your telephone call I did have a look to see who was on the desk on January fifth. There were two girls, both of whom are here now. Would you care to speak with them?"

"Thank you," said Ross. "That would be very helpful."

Cindy and Julia were summoned, but neither were able to identify the pictures of Ellis Martin that Ross had brought. He had to admit he was not surprised. It was, in fact, quite possible that Ellis had never even come here. If she had, the likelihood of either girl remembering her was remote. Colindale teemed with people from newspapers, schools, journals, all requesting and reading papers and microfiche on any possible subject from any possible date. At best, the chances of Ellis being remembered were slender.

After Julia and Cindy departed, the Head Librarian turned to Constable Marshall and said, "I'm terribly sorry, Constable, but I am afraid that now all I can offer you is the other alternative."

Ross had brought the unfortunate Constable Marshall with him for precisely this eventuality. Colindale, like most libraries of its kind, was not computerized. Requests were made and filed in slips giving the date, the name of the reader and the title and date of the requested periodical. Most likely, Ellis would have known exactly what she was looking for. If she had not, she would have used the huge index books in the front halls to find the periodicals that would have covered her subject. She then would have had to fill out request slips for each roll of microfiche or paper that she wished to see. These request slips were then filed in the basement of the building, presumably kept until the space filled up and then tossed. Unfortunately, the only way to establish whether or not she had been there and what she had been reading was to manually search through the files. This was to be the task of Constable Marshall. As he followed Marshall and the Head Librarian down to the basement, Ross thought the worthy constable was taking on the tiresome task with exceptionally good grace.

"I've set a room aside," the Head Librarian said, opening the door to a small office. There was a table and chair, a tiny window and some ten long filing boxes of slips. "I had them pull all of the files from January fifth. As you can see, there are rather a lot of them."

"You know what you're looking for?" asked Ross. Tom Marshall nodded. Ross was still well-known in the ranks of the Met. His legend had been enhanced by its overtones of money, romance, and tragedy. Tom Marshall was very much in awe of him. Marshall was also intelligent enough to realize that drudgery was a given in an investigation and he was determined that if the name "Ellis Martin" was among this slew of paper, he would locate it.

"I want to know as soon as you think you've got something, anything at all," Ross was saying. "I want you to telephone me directly. These are my numbers at home and in my car." He handed Marshall a slip of paper and smiled. "Good luck, Constable."

As he vanished through the door, Marshall took off his jacket, hung it over the back of his chair, and pulled the first box of slips toward him.

"Thank you for taking the time to see me," Ross said as he shook William DeWarre's hand. After leaving Constable Marshall to do battle with the request slips, Ross had come straight to the British Film Institute offices to keep the appointment that he had made that morning with William DeWarre.

DeWarre looked terrible and was obviously exhausted. The memory of sleepless nights and a desperate urge to keep busy enough not to think was all too familiar to Ross. Now DeWarre sat down at his desk and lit a cigarette. He offered one to Ross.

"No, thank you," Ross said, sitting down in the modular armchair.

"You don't mind if I do?" DeWarre asked. "It's a ghastly habit, I know. I've only taken it up again recently. I'd managed to quit completely, but you get this awful feeling that you have to do something with your hands."

"Yes, I know," said Ross.

"I'm afraid I'm a bit of a mess at the moment." DeWarre smiled weakly. "Excuse me. I've got the most god-awful amount of work to do, which is probably just as well. I'm glad you came. I'm sorry that I couldn't be more of a help on the telephone this morning. I've absolutely no idea why Ellis would have wanted to go to Colindale."

"I think I do," said Ross. "And if I'm right, we shall know quite soon. With a bit of luck, that is. However, I would like your help."

"Anything, of course."

"Did Ellis ever, to your recollection, talk to you about her parents, about where they came from, who they were, anything at all? Take your time, it could be important."

DeWarre looked out of the window. Then he shook his head and ground his cigarette out into the glass disc that served as an ashtray. "No, I can't remember her ever even mentioning them. She did talk about her aunt, of course, and about growing up in Wildesham. But I can't recall her ever talking about her parents at all. I never brought it up because I simply assumed that it was too painful."

"Can you help me with this, then?" Ross asked. "I have her diary here. Can you help me try to piece together what you did from, say, the first of January this year?" DeWarre nodded and reached into his desk drawer. He pulled out a diary and placed it on the desk.

"I'm afraid," he said, "that I'm one of those compulsive characters who writes everything down."

"Good," said Ross, "let's start with January first."

"Well, that's easy. We weren't even hung over. As a matter of fact, we were down in Wildesham. We stayed in New Year's Eve and on the first, the Sunday, we went for afternoon drinks at those people's—"

"Yes," said Ross, "I've got that here. The Ramsays' at half past twelve?"

"That's right," said DeWarre. "The whole village was there. Apparently it's something they do every year. It was very county, very dull. We stayed for all of an hour. Of course the by-election wasn't called until the twelfth, or something, but we joked about it later. If we'd known that she was going to be the next MP we'd of stayed and done some social climbing. Anyway, that afternoon we closed up the house and Ellis drove me back up here."

"According to Ellis's diary," said Ross, "you saw a film here on the second, you went to the cinema on the third, you went out to dinner on the fourth, and she went back down to Wildesham on the fifth? That is, after she went to Colindale, as we now know."

"Correct," said DeWarre.

"That weekend you went down to Wildesham and I have a note here that says, 'Mary and Ted.'"

"Mary and Ted Carrington, friends of mine. He works here. We'd invited them down for the weekend some time before but, as it turned out, they canceled. I went down anyway. And we did just about nothing, if I recall correctly. I think we may have gone to Tunbridge Wells to look at some possible curtain material."

"And you left on Sunday evening?"

"That's right," said DeWarre. "Ellis stayed down there, came up on Tuesday."

"On the tenth?"

"Yes. We were screening more films for the classic documentary series and I knew she wanted to see them. She'd got interested in documentary by then, or rather I'd got her interested in it. In any case, that night we saw two films from the archives here." He glanced at his diary. "They would have been 'Triumph of The Will' and the 'Titticut Follies.' A nice mixture of madness and fascism. As a matter of fact, that was the evening when Ellis got so interested in Leni

Riefenstahl, the German filmmaker I told you about. We went out to supper and talked about her afterward. I remember Ellis saying that she wanted to see 'Triumph' again. Anyway," he went on, "that was the tenth. The eleventh I have nothing and on the twelfth I have a note saying that I was going to meet Ellis here at half past ten that evening. I had a late meeting and she may well have come in and had something screened. In fact she did," he said, "I remember. And then I have nothing until the sixteenth. We screened two more documentaries here and I know that Ellis came to both of those. On the seventeenth I had to be late again and Ellis watched something in a screening booth, I don't know what. Nothing until the nineteenth when we had dinner with some friends at Ménage à Trois. On the twenty-fourth I have her going down to Wildesham and staying there until the twenty-sixth."

"Yes, that's here as well," said Ross.

"She came back up on the evening of the twenty-sixth because we had a dinner to go to," DeWarre went on. "On the twenty-seventh I had to work late and I think Ellis just stayed home rather than coming to meet me. On the twenty-eighth we went to the theater, on Sunday we lazed about the flat, and on the thirtieth I was working like a fiend and that sums up January. She drove me to the airport on the morning of the first."

He shut the diary and pushed it aside. "I'm sorry, Chief Inspector," he said. "It all seemed terribly normal to me. Perhaps if I hadn't been working so hard I would have noticed whatever there was to notice."

"No," said Ross. "It may well be that there was

nothing to notice at all. I simply wanted to be certain. There is just one thing, however. On the nights that Ellis had films screened for herself, the twelfth and the seventeenth, do you know what she saw?"

"No," said DeWarre, "but I can easily find out. Do you think it could be important?" He picked up his telephone.

"I don't know," said Ross. He didn't want to admit he was grasping at straws.

"Susie," said DeWarre, "could you come in for a minute?" He hung up and a moment later a tall thin girl with what looked like vaseline on her hair opened the door. "Susie," DeWarre asked, "do you remember what film Ellis asked for on the night of Jan twelve and Jan seventeen?"

She looked at Ross for a moment and then she said, "No, but I can look it up."

"Would you?" DeWarre asked. She nodded and disappeared. A moment later the telephone rang. DeWarre listened for a moment, raised his eyebrows and thanked someone whom Ross presumed to be "Susie." He hung up the phone and turned back to Ross. "Well," he said, "on both the night of the twelfth and the night of the seventeenth, Ellis watched the BBC film on Briarcliffe." Ross sat forward in his chair.

"Had she seen it before, do you know?" he asked.

"Yes," said DeWarre. "She first saw it with me on January second. It was the film we saw here that night. I remember because it was the first of the series that we screened. I had no idea that it had made such an impression on her."

"So, she saw it the first time with you on the second, you screened it for her on the twelfth, and she requested it again on the seventeenth?" And in the meantime, thought Ross, unless I am very much mistaken, she went off to visit the newspaper archives at Colindale. "Do you think," Ross asked, "that it might be possible to arrange for me to see the Briarcliffe film?"

The BBC documentary of Briarcliffe was very grim indeed. It was also nearly three hours long in its uncut version, and since that was what Ellis had watched, it was also what Ross watched. It covered the history of asylums in Britain, the history of Briarcliffe itself, and the history of the Clara Beale case. The film had not been approved by the Department of Health and Social Services and the administration at Briarcliffe had not cooperated. As a result, there was a lot of footage of people scurrying between cars and buildings that had been taken from a great distance and, in some cases, from behind a hedge. There were interviews with doctors, nurses, and secretaries whose faces were not shown and some footage had even been shot from a helicopter. In one sequence, a group of men and women started to come out of the front of the building, got halfway down the vast stone steps, saw the film crew, and turned and fled. The film crew pursued them around the corner of the terrace where they hid in a utility shed and shouted, "go away" and "leave us alone" through the wooden slatted doorway. It might have been pathetic, or even funny, if the story hadn't been so overwhelmingly horrible. The picture of Clara Beale appeared several times and each time Ross felt his stomach heave at the sight of her clear, childish face and the thought of what her woman's body and uncomprehending baby mind had been forced to suffer.

After the first hour of human misery, madness, and "Victorian" treatments, Ross began to feel worn. By the end of the third hour of the bleak Yorkshire moors, torture, imprisonment, injustice, and agony, he was exhausted. It occurred to him as he finally left the Institute that his fatigue might also have to do with the fact that it was well past midnight.

As he turned onto the M25 and headed home, Ross wondered if he were losing his touch. There had been nothing of use to him in the Briarcliffe film, nothing he could see in any case. And despite the exhaustion, he had looked hard. He had to admit that he couldn't begin to imagine why it was that Ellis Martin had wanted to see the damn thing three times. Of course, DeWarre's prognosis could be correct. It could simply be that once something interested her, she went overboard. Or, perhaps she was simply bats, thought Ross. Or she had developed a passionate interest in asylums and was going to apply for planning permission to build one in Wildesham, with Mr. Dawling and the planning board her first unwilling inmates. After dynamiting the depot, of course.

By the time he turned into his driveway he had to admit that he was, at that moment, too tired to care if Ellis Martin had been formulating plans to blow up the whole of Kent. It was a quarter of two in the morning and all that he wanted to do was go to bed.

He heard the telephone before he had the front door open. His first thought was that it was poor Constable Marshall who had uncovered a goldmine of pertinent information and hadn't dared to go to bed until he informed Ross personally. He flicked on the front hall lights and ran across the darkened sitting room to the telephone. The voice on the other end was not that of

Tom Marshall, subdued with terror, but Owen. And he was bloody annoyed.

"Oh," said Ross, none too cheerful himself, "what the hell do you want?"

"To know where the hell you've been," Owen said. "It's a quarter to two in the bloody morning!"

"Yes," said Ross, "so I am aware. As a matter of fact, I've been to a very long film."

"Any good?" asked Owen.

"No," Ross said. "God-awful. I don't know what the hell Ellis Martin was or wasn't up to, but I don't share her taste in cinema."

"Well, I shouldn't think you'll have to worry about it anymore," said Owen. "In fact, you can sleep tight. We've found the car in a rental agency just this side of Maidstone, and they've identified Dawling from a photo as the man who rented it."

Chapter

18

•

It was rented from 'Castle Garage and Rentals' in
Bearsted on the morning of February fourth," announced Owen.

The file sat on Ross's desk where it had been waiting
for him when he came in. Owen, however, had no
need to refer to it. Ross wondered if he'd slept with it
under his pillow, implanting it word for word in his
brain.

"It had been booked by telephone a few days
before," Owen continued, "in the name of a Mr.
Thompson. Inventive, isn't he?"

"The soul of originality," said Ross. "Go on."

"Mr. Thompson, A.K.A. Kenneth Dawling, arrived
to collect the car at half past nine on the morning of
the fourth. It was a day rental for which he paid in
cash. Twenty-five quid as well, little thieves that Castle
Rentals are." Owen was obviously enjoying himself.

"How did he get there?" asked Ross. "To collect it, I
mean."

"He was driven by a man in a blue car, which may or may not have been a Triumph. The same man followed him back that evening when he returned the car at about six."

"And his alibi for the afternoon of the fourth?"

"Well, he says that he was in and out of his offices and garages all day. But I should think we'll be able to knock a hole in that without too much trouble," Owen said, grinning. "Of course," he continued, "I couldn't believe it when I got up there after hearing from this sharp lad at Maidstone that they had a couple of Rovers that they rented and that one of them was white. They've only got about a half a dozen cars and there she was, right as rain. There was no sign of a GBH on the license plates, but I thought I'd give it a whirl in any case. They went and identified Dawling straightaway, both the owner and his wife. Remembered him on account of his charming manner."

"Of course," said Ross.

He pulled the file toward him and flipped it open. After perusing the first page for a moment, he glanced up at Owen.

"The car hasn't been taken out again since the fourth?"

"Amazing, isn't it?" Owen was positively beaming with pleasure. "I never thought our luck would break on this bloody case. I honestly didn't." He glanced at his watch and nodded with satisfaction. "We should hear the preliminary reports from forensics this afternoon. They had it out of there faster than you could say, well, whatever it is that you say in these circumstances."

Ross closed the file and smiled at him. "Congratulations, Owen," he said. "You've every reason to look like the cat that ate the cheese."

"I think it's milk, Master," Owen said, a look of momentary concern for Ross's mental health passing over his face. "But the cat was a Cheshire, the one in Alice I mean," he added as a consolation prize.

"Oh, whatever," said Ross, unfolding himself stiffly from his chair. It occurred to him that, with any luck, he wouldn't have to be in this wretched chair in this wretched office for very much longer. The plastic clock over the door told him that it was half past noon. "Let us retreat to the Cavendish House where I will buy you lunch and we shall drink a bottle of wine," he said. He was suddenly feeling uncharacteristically jolly at the idea of Kenneth Dawling behind bars and his imminent escape from the Millbrook police station. Stale donuts, nasty coffee, and bolshy witnesses would all be left in his wake.

Owen, looking mildly startled, got to his feet.

"I take it," said Ross, reaching for his overcoat, "that you are keeping a discreet eye on friend Dawling?"

"Oh yes," said Owen. "I don't want to put the cat among the pigeons, but he won't leave town without our knowing. You didn't want me to do anything until we had the forensics reports in? After all, Master, it's not actually illegal to rent a white Rover."

"Alas no," said Ross. "But it would be most unfortunate if he decided, for some reason best known to himself, to do a runner just now."

"He's not going anywhere," said Owen, buttoning up his coat. "In so far as he knows, not a thing is going on."

"Good!" said Ross as he vigorously swung the door of his office open.

"Constable Glen," he said as he strode past the front desk with Owen trotting behind him. "Forward all urgent calls to the dining room of the Cavendish Hotel."

The call from the forensics team did not come during lunch. Nor did it come during the remainder of the afternoon. Ross himself hated waiting for anything, but he knew it would be far worse for Owen, who would deserve the lion's share of the credit when forensics rang with the expected news. At least the three-course lunch and bottle of Beaune had helped to while away the time.

Personally, Ross felt like something of an ass over this case and he would not be sorry when it was over. While Owen had been following a perfectly rational path, getting the inevitably rational results, Ross had been rushing about, chasing his tail in such idiotic places as Colindale and the British Film Institute.

He knew Owen suspected what he'd been up to, but was grateful his colleague didn't actually know. Ross found the whole history of his juvenile behavior on this case faintly embarrassing. It had begun with his temper tantrum over Kate Davidson not telling him about Ellis's pregnancy and had continued apace with his obsession about the planning permission and some devious plot being cooked up by Ellis Martin.

If it did turn out that Dawling had killed her, as it probably would, it would likely be because he was an unbalanced minor lunatic who had taken a grudge one step too far, whacking Ellis Martin on the head in a fit of temper simply because she'd been nasty about his wretched depot.

The telephone rang. Ross pounced on it, hoping it would be good news.

"Chief Inspector Ross?" asked the polite voice on the other end.

"Yes," said Ross.

"Constable Marshall here, sir," said the voice. "You said that I was to notify you personally as soon as I found anything?"

Ross started to tell Constable Thomas Marshall not to bother. He had, unfortunately, been the victim of a bad practical joke, but Ross didn't have the heart. Constable Marshall need never know that his boring hours in the basement of the Colindale library had been futile.

"Yes, Constable Marshall," he said, trying to sound enthusiastic. "What have you got for me?"

"Well," said Thomas Marshall. "She was there all right, sir, on January fifth. She must have been there nearly all day. She pulled some ten separate periodicals and papers, sir. And all of them dealt with a scandal at a mental hospital in Yorkshire called Briarcliffe."

"I see," said Ross. He was hardly surprised.

"She also pulled several pieces on the Department of Health and Social Services and on the subsequent enquiry," Constable Marshall was saying. "I have a list of everything here, sir," he continued. "Shall I write up a report for you?"

"Yes, absolutely. That's very good work, Constable. You've been a great help."

Ross made a note on his pad to remember to recommend Constable Marshall for something desirable the next time the opportunity arose.

After he hung up, Ross did give himself the very

minor satisfaction of a small mental pat on the back. Unless the whole thing turned upside down at the eleventh hour, Kate Davidson hadn't killed Ellis Martin. He was pleased about that. For her sake, of course. He was glad that David Grainger was very probably not a murderer either. "Now they can get married and live happily ever after and won't that be nice?" he said to himself.

He opened the desk drawer and took out the box containing Billy's earring. Perhaps it did belong to Mrs. Dawling and had fallen out of Dawling's pocket as he committed the wicked deed. Perhaps she was his accomplice and had lost it there herself. Perhaps it belonged to someone who had rented the car before Dawling and had later gotten scuffed out into the leaves of Tinker Wood. Perhaps it belonged to none of these people and meant nothing at all, in which case it could be returned to Billy Carter to take its place as the jewel of his treasure trove.

"Toodle Pip," Ross said out loud as he dropped it back into its box.

"And to you."

Owen was standing in the doorway. Ross could see that he was so excited that he could barely contain himself. He came in and shut the door behind him.

"They've found traces of blood under the rug in the boot and a couple of blond hairs as well as some clothing fibers. They'll be able to say for certain tomorrow morning whether or not they belong to Ellis Martin."

"Congratulations," said Ross. Owen was positively beaming.

"He, or they, had a right good go at cleaning it up,

let me tell you. You know how head wounds bleed. But they weren't quite thorough enough."

"No," said Ross. "Mind you, it's the ones who are thorough enough that we never hear about. What time is it now?" he asked.

"Half five," said Owen. "They said they'd be able to tell us by 9:00 A.M. tomorrow morning."

"Fine," said Ross, standing up. "Put someone else on to watch him tonight, just to be certain. We'll bring him in tomorrow morning as soon as we have the report. You should be proud of yourself, Owen." He added, "Give the lovely Miranda a kiss for me and get a good night's sleep. Tomorrow's going to be a long day."

The envelope lying on the front desk had Ross's name clearly printed across the front. Without thinking, Ross picked it up as he was on his way out to go home. He waved it at Owen as he got into his car.

Ross was exhausted by the time he arrived home. You're getting older, he said to himself. These days you can't go rushing about until two in the morning without feeling it. He wondered if, when Ellis Martin was all taken care of, he might not take a vacation. A week at Gleneagles to catch the spring fishing seemed quite appealing. But that would not be until at least the end of the month. What I need now, he thought, is a stiff whiskey. Dropping his overcoat on the hall chair, he made for the sitting room.

Barry Glen felt even more self-important than usual as he dialed the telephone number where Angie worked. He didn't usually ring her at work, not as a rule. It wasn't as much that they minded, even if they were a bit hoity-toity. It was more that he didn't consider it professional. Still, this evening it was a necessity. It was very likely that he wouldn't be home all night and he couldn't just let her worry. And besides, he was dying to tell someone that he was being sent to watch over a murder suspect who was about to be arrested.

"Arrested!" Angie exclaimed, "Ken Dawling! Well, I never!"

"Sssh! For heaven's sake, Angie," Barry hissed into the telephone. "You mustn't go about saying anything. This is official police business. You're not to tell a soul, you hear? I shouldn't even be telling you, but I didn't want you to worry an' all."

"I'm sorry," Angie said, "I'm sorry, love. It's only that it's, well, so terrible. When is it then—tonight?"

"I don't know," Barry said. "But I may not be home at all and you're not to worry yourself."

"Well, I will," said Angie. "I was going to be late myself, what with this job," she added. "Now you take care, Barry Glen."

"Don't worry about me, pet," Barry said, feeling positively inflated with his own importance. "I must go now."

"Right ho, Barry," Angie said.

As she hung up the telephone she saw her employer standing in the doorway. "Oh, I am sorry," Angie said, blushing. "He doesn't usually telephone me here. It was only to say that he wasn't going to get home tonight. You can't imagine what a policeman's job is like," she added.

It wasn't until after he had changed his clothes and lit the fire that Ross remembered the envelope. He had dropped it onto the chair in the front hall along with his coat. There hardly seemed any point in reading it now, but he nonetheless took it back to his sitting room with him. I suppose that most decent men are spending their Monday evenings at dinner parties or at the theater or playing with their children, Ross thought. I, on the other hand, am idling it away drinking whiskey and sorting through the mail of a dead woman.

The dead woman's mail consisted of several flyers from Greenpeace and a notice from the local land-owner's committee. Also in the envelope was a large, brown, stiff-backed mail package. It was the type used to mail photographs and it was addressed to "Chief Inspector Ross." Ross put the landowner's notice aside and opened the photo package.

It was from Harry Matchum. Inside there was a note which simply said, "Here are the pictures of some of the principals, as promised. Let me know if I can be of further help—Harry."

Ross slipped the pictures out of their cardboard folder and read the caption on the first one. It said, simply, "The Beale Family, 1963." Ross turned it over and looked at the slightly blurry black and white photo. In it, Mr. and Mrs. Beale stood in front of a small semi-detached house with their children clustered around them. Clara clutched her mother's hand. She was smiling. Ross put the photo aside. The caption on the next photograph read, "staff, Briarcliffe, 1971." Again in black and white, the nurses, doctors, and orderlies of Briarcliffe lined up on the steps below the terrace of the main house. Ross pulled the last photo from the package. The caption read, "L—Head Floor Supervisor, Diane Ness. R—

Nurse Jane Trew—caught unaware. Both on duty the night of C.B.'s death. Should have been prosecuted, case dropped. Them sacked."

Ross flipped the picture over. It was a high quality eight-by-ten glossy, taken, probably, with a telephoto lens. Two women stood on either side of a small car. They were both wearing staff nursing uniforms. The woman on the right, Jane Trew, looked away from the camera and only her profile was visible. The woman on the left, Diane Ness, had been caught looking directly into the lens.

For a moment Ross stared at the photograph in his hand and it was then that he finally understood where Ellis Martin had been leading him, saw what she had seen and knew why it was that she had sat through three showings of "Briarcliffe."

Chapter

19

Ross nearly kicked over his whiskey glass as he jumped for the telephone. He knew Owen's number by heart, but tonight it took forever to dial. After what seemed to be a very long time, but was in fact only four rings, Miranda answered the telephone.

"Miranda, it's Ross," he said. "Please can you get me Owen, quickly?"

Ross could hear her footsteps echoing down the polished floor of the hallway, hear her raised voice calling for Owen. A moment later he picked up the telephone.

"Master?" Owen asked.

"You've got someone watching Dawling's house?"

"Glen's down there in a plain car, along with some other youngblood whose name I always forget. Why?"

"Good," said Ross, ignoring his question. "I hate to do this to you," he went on, "but I want you to meet me at the station. No," he corrected himself, "there isn't time for that. Meet me at Dawling's house and for Christ's sake, hurry. I'm leaving now." And before Owen could ask him anything else he put the phone down and ran from the house.

The twenty-five-minute drive would surely go on forever. Ross looked at his dashboard clock. It was just a quarter to. With luck he could be there by seven.

He could be wrong. There could be no emergency whatsoever. But his instincts told him otherwise. He wondered how Ellis had first gotten onto it and supposed that it was just the highly developed instinct of a good troublemaker. Well, this time she'd made some trouble for herself, all right.

He cursed himself for being so infernally thick as to have missed so completely where it was that she was leading him. Ellis had been cleverer than anyone had given her credit for. Now he just hoped he wouldn't be too late to stop the whole thing from turning into a total catastrophe.

He drove straight through Wildesham toward The Hall and turned into the side lane where the Dawlings lived. He could see a car ahead of him on the road and he pulled up behind it and stopped. Owen appeared at his window and he looked worried.

"Dawling's hopped it," he said.

"What?" Ross opened the door and got out.

It was very dark and a thin rain was falling, making the tarmac glisten in the headlights. A young constable, whom he recognized from the front desk, materialized from out of the dark beside Owen.

"I didn't think you'd be so fast, sir," he said.

"What happened?" asked Ross.

"Dawling left here in his car a few minutes ago, sir," said the constable. "We were told to keep out of the way and not to interfere," he said, nervously glancing at Owen.

"Go on," Owen said.

"I'm certain he didn't see us," he continued. "Barry, Constable Glen that is, followed him in the car and left me here to watch the house. He was calling in for instructions."

"Is there anyone in the house?" Ross asked. The constable nodded.

"I think Mrs. Dawling, sir. We could see when he stopped under the gate light. I'm certain that he was alone."

"Quick," said Ross to Owen as he started up the drive toward the house. Owen followed, leaving the constable at the gate.

Mrs. Dawling opened the front door on the second ring. She started to say something but she didn't have time before Ross cut her off.

"Mrs. Dawling," he said, "I'm the police. We have to know where your husband's gone."

"Why?" she asked, a stubborn line appearing in the set of her small red-painted mouth.

"It's vital, Mrs. Dawling!" Ross was nearly shouting. "Please!" She looked slightly startled at the tone of his voice and then a small tinge of fear crept into her face.

"The garages," she said. "About ten minutes ago he got a phone call. He said he had to nip down to the garage. There's not—" But before she could finish the question Ross had turned and raced back down the drive, Owen in pursuit.

"Get in!" Ross shouted at Owen, gesturing toward the passenger side of his car. "You stay where you are," he called to the increasingly bewildered constable. Then he and Owen backed into the Dawlings' drive and, with a screech of tires, disappeared down the lane in the direction of Wildesham.

There was no traffic on the road. A good thing, thought Owen, because Ross was driving at a speed that could be categorized as demented.

"What in the hell is going on?" Owen gasped.

"I hope I don't know," Ross said. "I hope to hell I'm wrong." They reached the crossroads and turned west toward Ellis's house and the Dawling garages.

The police car was parked in the road outside of the garage entrance. Ross drove straight past it and into the parking area. He pulled up beside the red Ford Owen recognized as Dawling's. A light was on in the office, glowing behind drawn curtains. As the policemen rushed from the car, Barry Glen appeared out of the rain.

"Is he inside?" Ross asked.

Barry nodded.

"I thought I ought to try to follow and watch him, sir."

"Good," said Ross. "Have you seen anyone else?"

Barry shook his head and before he could answer there was a crashing sound from inside the office.

"No! Police!" Ross shouted as he sprinted toward the office door with Owen and Barry behind him.

The garage's office appeared to be empty. Ross hesitated for a moment before he spotted the open door in the far wall behind the desk. It could only lead into the servicing sheds beyond.

Ross nearly tripped over Dawling. He lay just beyond the doorway in the entrance to the shed. In the pool of light streaming from the office, Ross could see a dark puddle of blood seeping around his head and shoulders. He stood back as Owen jumped across the body and disappeared into the shed.

Dawling had pulled a filing cabinet over as he fell and his legs were trapped beneath. That, thought Ross, was the crashing noise that had, hopefully, saved his life.

Barry Glen stood in the office doorway, his mouth agape. Ross knelt down next to Dawling. "Get an ambulance," he said, "and say a prayer that he's not dead."

Owen returned a few minutes later. He was breathing hard and his shoes and the bottom of his trousers were muddy. "Out the back there," he said. "There's a door that was open. Gives on to some woods and one hell of a lot of mud. We scared them off, all right, but they'll not get far."

"No," said Ross.

"I'll go put out a bulletin, get everyone in here," Owen said, stepping over Dawling and heading for the office.

"He's not dead," said Ross, standing up. "You stay here with him and Glen. Find something to keep him warm." He walked back into the office where Barry was just hanging up the telephone.

"On their way," Barry said. "Is he—?"

"No," said Ross.

"Where are you going?" asked Owen. Ross looked at him and smiled.

"To pay a social call," he said.

He could have walked, but decided to drive. The house was lit and the cars had been put in the garage. Ross stood in the rain waiting for someone to answer the front door.

The man who came to the door was wearing a tweed jacket and an old school tie. Ross felt a momentary pang of guilt and hoped they weren't planning to go out. Not that it mattered, he thought. Once again, he was about to ruin someone's evening.

After introducing himself, he was invited inside. The house was cozy after the rain.

"I'm terribly sorry to bother you," Ross said, "but I'm afraid that I need to speak with your wife."

"Of course, Chief Inspector," he said. "We're actually having people in to supper. Perhaps you could join us? Just a moment," he continued. "I believe she's upstairs changing." He went to the bottom of the stairs and called up. There was no reply.

Ross heard the sound of a door closing and a woman's voice called, "Just coming, darling."

"Ah," her husband said, "she'll be right with us. Won't you come into the sitting room?" But Ross was already walking down the hall toward the kitchen.

She was standing on the mat inside the kitchen door taking off a pair of wellingtons. Ross supposed that she must have dumped the mac and perhaps a pair of gloves in the garage. Her dark velvet dress showed no sign that she had recently been outside, nor did her hair, which, Ross thought, had probably been covered with a scarf, now also deposited in the garage. The same familiar-looking blond girl stood by the kitchen table where she was arranging a tray of hors d'oeuvres.

"Chief Inspector," Mrs. Ramsay said, smiling, "what an unexpected pleasure."

Ross had to give her credit. She was as cool as they came, not a hair out of place.

"Oh, there you are," her husband said, coming up behind him. "Do come and have a drink."

"Yes," she said. "I do hope you'll join us. Forgive me, I just had to lock the dog up. She's a bitch on heat, such a frightful bore. Angela, bring the glasses into the sitting room, would you?"

"It's all right, Mrs. Ramsay," Ross said. "He's not dead." She widened her eyes and smiled.

"I'm afraid I have no idea what you mean," she said.

"Kenneth Dawling is going to be fine," Ross said. "I should think you've broken his collar bone and his legs may be broken as well. He's had rather a nasty bump on the head, but that's the extent of it. I'm afraid your aim wasn't quite so accurate this time."

She stared at him and for a moment Ross almost felt sorry for her. He saw the thought of the kitchen door going through her mind, and he shook his head sadly.

"That won't do much good," he said. "There are rather a lot of policemen out there. Now," he continued, dropping his voice so that it became almost gentle, "at the risk of being very boring, I'm going to ask you again to tell me about Ellis Martin."

Chapter

20.

So Diane Ness and Laura Ramsay are the same person?" Mary Jepp asked. She filled the Inspector's wineglass once more.

"That's right," said Ross. "After Briarcliffe, Diane Ness changed her name to Laura Braithe. It was done by deed poll in York. She set out to build a new life for herself."

"And she succeeded admirably," said Sam. "Until Ellis."

"Yes," said Ross. "For twenty years things had gone along swimmingly for Laura Braithe Ramsay. Until Ellis happened to see an old documentary on Briarcliffe."

"Was she so very recognizable?" asked Mary. Ross shook his head.

"I missed her altogether," he confessed. "At least the first time. I've seen the pertinent bit since and she is there, but it was just dumb luck that Ellis recognized her the first time. Of course afterward she followed her instincts to Colindale and then she got onto Matchum and viewed the film again."

Ross, David Grainger, and the Jepps had just finished a leg of spring lamb and now they sat in the Jepps' dining room polishing off a delightful bottle of chardonnay. It was Sunday and the case had been closed for nearly a week. Dawling, now recovering nicely in hospital, had obligingly told the police everything he knew the moment he had come to. In the end, he hadn't actually known much of anything and, by the time he made his dramatic confession, it was largely redundant. Laura Ramsay, knowing when the game was up, had agreed to assist the police with their enquiries. By 5:00 P.M. on Wednesday she had been officially charged with the killing of Ellis Martin.

"And Ellis was blackmailing her?" Mary asked.

"In a manner of speaking," said Ross. "She first approached Laura Ramsay in early January. She told her what she knew and she also told her that she'd keep quiet about it if Laura threw her weight behind reversing the haulage depot decision."

"Could she do that, even if she'd wanted to?" David asked. "I mean Laura," he added.

"I doubt it," said Ross. "Once those decisions are made they're out of the hands of the council. I really doubt that there would have been anything at all that Mrs. Ramsay could have done. Apparently she tried to explain that to Ellis, but to no avail."

"Ellis wouldn't have believed her," said David. "She was always quite certain that you could get your own way if you tried hard enough."

"In any case," Ross continued, "Laura Ramsay was playing for time, which was fine until January twelfth."

"Oh Christ," said Sam, "the by-election."

"That's right," said Ross. "Suddenly Laura was a candidate for Parliament. Everything that she'd worked for was coming true."

"And there was Ellis Martin holding a stick of dynamite beneath her," said Mary.

"That's right," said Ross. "Laura had invested twenty years in getting rid of Diane Ness. She simply couldn't afford to have her come back again."

"So she decided to kill her," Sam said.

"Apparently Ellis was upping the pressure, threatening to go to the press. Being Diane Ness certainly wasn't illegal, but it would have destroyed Laura Ramsay just as her greatest dream was in reach."

"How did she do it?" Mary asked.

"Well," said Ross. "She knew about the film course because Ellis had talked about it at the cocktail party on New Year's Day. The same with DeWarre going to Spain. She was able to choose her time. After that it was simplicity itself. She asked Dawling to rent the car for her on some excuse about her husband's being serviced. He was more than happy to do anything at all for his great champion in arms, particularly since she was going to be an MP. This time, unfortunately, his crawling got him into rather a lot of trouble. Once he'd rented the car he was an accessory. If he ever put two and two together and worked out what she'd used it for, no one was going to believe him when he said he didn't know what was going on. So he was stuck. She put the car in the garage and then she went to Ellis's house by the footpath on Friday afternoon. Everyone in the village knew Mrs. Jeffers didn't work that day. Laura waited until Ellis appeared and then persuaded her to walk back to Laurel House. She got her into the garage, hit her on the head with the spade, put her into the car and took her to Tinker Wood."

"It would never have occurred to Ellis that anyone would actually hurt her," David said. "She just flew in and out of people's lives."

"And the scarf?" asked Sam.

"A nice touch," said Ross, "added simply to muddy the waters. Mrs. Ramsay saw it the last time she was in Harvey Nichols."

"So she'd been planning this for some time?" Mary asked.

"Oh yes," said Ross. "Almost as soon as the by-election was called and she knew that she'd be a candidate. She planned it very carefully. And if she hadn't been just a little bit too clever and changed the license plates on the rental car with an old set from her garage, we might never have caught her. Kate would never have remembered the car if those plates hadn't been on it."

"The memory of Katherine Davidson is as peculiar as everything else about her," said Mary, smiling. "I did ask her to join us today," she added, "but she's apparently held hostage in her studio."

"I take it," said David, "that Laura took the spade from the farm while she was wandering about with the planning board looking at the specs for the milking parlor."

"That's right," said Ross. "They visited several times. Of course, she needed a weapon that couldn't be traced to her and it did serve to confuse things even further."

"And what about Billy's lovely earring?" Mary asked. "Ellis's?"

"As a matter of fact, no," said Ross. "And it didn't

belong to Laura Ramsay either. I don't suppose we'll ever know how it got there. It's been returned to Billy. His father has put it in the bank for him. The stone's been valued at about £100."

"Oh God," Mary said suddenly. "She had no idea what she was up against, did she? I mean Ellis. She was just playing. She was just angry about a haulage depot." Mary pushed her chair away from the table and went quickly into the kitchen. After a moment, Ross followed her.

She was placing cups and saucers for coffee on a tray. If it had not been for the slight shaking of her shoulders, he would not have known she was crying. She placed a sugar bowl carefully on the tray and then she looked up at him. "We weren't very kind to her," she said. "I mean, I just can't help wondering. If we'd been kinder, if we'd paid a little more attention—"

"Don't," said Ross. "It doesn't help."

"Yes it does," Mary said. "Perhaps from now on we'll all try a little harder."

Ross stayed for a cup of coffee before excusing himself just after 4:00 P.M. There was one more call that he wanted to make. The rain had stopped in the middle of the week and the weather was disconcertingly warm again. The daffodils had emerged along The Hall's back drive. At this rate, thought Ross, they'll be gone by Easter and we'll be heading into summer by May Day.

Ross parked his car behind the garage and walked across the lawn to Kate's studio. She called to him to come in before he had a chance to knock on the door.

Sitting on a high stool at her drafting table, she turned and smiled at him from under a cloud of unruly hair. The triptych was finished and the lions and leopards peeped out from among the flowers.

"I've come to say good-bye," he said, suddenly feeling rather silly. She put her pencil down and pushed the hair out of her eyes.

"I'm sorry I couldn't join you all for lunch," she said. "I'm a bit behind. I'm working on a theater set design. It's not the sort of thing I usually do, but this one's actually quite interesting."

"I'm glad," he said. "You look less tired."

Kate got down off her stool. "I'm getting a bit more sleep now that you don't suspect me of having whacked my childhood friend over the head with a spade."

"I never did suspect you," Ross said.

She smiled. "Chief Inspector," she said. "Something tells me that that's a highly unprofessional statement."

Ross was embarrassed to find himself blushing. It was time to go. He reached out to shake her hand. "Good luck, Kate," he said. "I'll look for you in the arts pages."

"I'll walk you to your car," she said, opening the door. "Tell me," she asked as they were crossing the lawn, "what do you do now?"

"The next case," said Ross.

"Another bashing on the head?"

"Perhaps," he replied. "Such is the policeman's lot. What about you? Are you going to be Mrs. David Grainger?"

She looked at him and laughed.

"I shouldn't depend on that at all, Chief Inspector."

They had reached the car and he put out his hand again. This time she took it.

"Tell me one more thing," she said, smiling. "Do you have another name, other than Chief Inspector Ross?" This time he knew she could see he was blushing.

"Hubert Walter," he said.

"I can see why you use Ross," she laughed. "It's been nice to meet you, Ross."

"Now that Mrs. Ramsay's no longer running," he said, opening his door, "perhaps the Alliance will get in and stop the depot." Kate looked toward the line of trees.

"Yes," she said quietly. "That was what Ellis wanted."

"Kate," Ross said suddenly. She looked at him. "Perhaps," he began. "Perhaps some time—"

She smiled.

"Yes, Ross," she answered. "Perhaps." And then she turned and walked back across the lawn toward her studio.